Dead Push
(Kiera Hudson Series Two)
Book 7

Tim O'Rourke

ISBN: 10:1492183202
ISBN-13:978-1492183204

Story Editor (Hacker)
Lynda O'Rourke
Book cover designed by:
Tim O'Rourke
Copyedited by:
Carolyn M. Pinard
Carolynpinardconsults@gmail.com

Happy Birthday to the 'Kiera Hudson Fanzine' competition winner

Courtney Jackson!

Thanks to:

Shana at bookvacations.wordpress.com
Braine & Cimmaron at Talkingsupe.com
Nikki Archer at vampsandstuff.com
Bella at paranormal book club
Suemcg-delirium.blogspot.com
Caroline Barker at Areadersreviewblog.wordpress.com
Melly at the Vampire Forum
Who all took the time to review my books – Thank you!

You can contact Tim O'Rourke at

www.kierahudson.com

Or by email at Kierahudson91@aol.com

More books by Tim O'Rourke

Kiera Hudson Series

Vampire Shift (Kiera Hudson Series 1) Book 1
Vampire Wake (Kiera Hudson Series 1) Book 2
Vampire Hunt (Kiera Hudson Series 1) Book 3
Vampire Breed (Kiera Hudson Series 1) Book 4
Wolf House (Kiera Hudson Series 1) Book 4.5
Vampire Hollows (Kiera Hudson Series 1) Book 5
Dead Flesh (Kiera Hudson Series 2) Book 1
Dead Night (Kiera Hudson Series 2) Book 1.5
Dead Angels (Kiera Hudson Series 2) Book 2
Dead Statues (Kiera Hudson Series 2) Book 3
Dead Seth (Kiera Hudson Series 2) Book 4
Dead Wolf (Kiera Hudson Series 2) Book 5
Dead Water (Kiera Hudson Series 2) Book 6

Black Hill Farm (Books 1 & 2)
Black Hill Farm (Book 1)
Black Hill Farm: Andy's Diary (Book 2)

Sydney Hart Novels
Witch (A Sydney Hart Novel) Book 1
Yellow (A Sydney Hart Novel) Book 2

The Doorways Trilogy

Doorways (Doorways Trilogy Book 1)
The League of Doorways (Doorways Trilogy Book 2)

Moon Trilogy
Moonlight (Moon Trilogy) Book 1
Moonbeam (Moon Trilogy) Book 2

<u>Samantha Carter – Vampire Seeker Series</u>
Vampire Seeker (Samantha Carter Series) Book 1

You can contact Tim O'Rourke at
www.kierahudson.com or by email at kierahudson91@aol.com

Dead Push

Chapter One

Potter

We were led by three wolves through the long stone corridors and back towards the custody block beneath Wasp Water Police Station. Jack walked beside me, head bent low on his scrawny neck. His long, drawn face looked more emaciated than I'd ever seen before. He was looking tired and old. He had been back in this *pushed* world for two hundred years – so I guess he had every right to be fraying around the edges. His long arms didn't swing loosely by his sides like they so often did, as his wrists were manacled behind him, as were mine. Jack stared down, rays of bright orange light seeping from his eyes and onto the stone floor, as if lighting our way through the intricate maze of stone corridors we were being led through. His stare was fixed and I wondered what the murderous giant was thinking. I had seen him kill those wolves in the room above, and even by my own standards his actions had been savage – way beyond anything I had seen before. He had ripped the flesh and fur from those wolves like some kind of crazed butcher. But he had saved me. Why? Jack had said he had done so not for me – but for his sister – *Kiera*. Jack said he hadn't wanted Luke Bishop to use me as bait to trap her. Kiera had gotten to him – she had managed, somehow, to get beneath his weather-beaten, wrinkled skin. If anyone could change Jack Seth, maybe prod at his rancid, black heart – it would be Kiera. Was this another gift she had – just like her ability to *see*? I didn't think so. Kiera's special gift was making you *see* things differently. Kiera was petite and beautiful. She didn't look strong or scary – but she had this other kind of strength. Kiera was like one of those fucking kids' toys – a *Weeble* – it didn't matter how many times you pushed her over – she always got up again. She had more fucking bounce than a rubber ball. But it was more than that – she wouldn't be turned, either – manipulated – or *pushed*. It was like she had this inner compass, but instead of having a 'north' point, hers always pointed in the direction of what was right – the most honest thing to do. And it didn't seem to matter however much she was spun around and *pushed* off course – Kiera always did what was right, even if it meant that she would suffer herself somehow.

I hadn't always understood that, but as I now walked to my death beside this brutal, savage killer of women and children, I could see that she had gotten to him. Jack had claimed many times he wanted to beat the Lycanthrope curse, and to do that he had to stop his killing, but this had always eluded him. He had never been able to kick the habit. But he had saved me – or *tried* to. It didn't matter whether I lived or died from this moment on – what mattered was the fact that he had tried. Had he ever tried to save a life before? Probably not. Whatever had happened between Jack and Kiera while he held her hostage in that house at the top of the hill, it had started a change deep within Jack. Had he hoped to have broken her in that house? I guessed that had been his plan. But it was Kiera who had broken Jack, even though she had been his prisoner. Perhaps she had got him to *see* stuff differently – to *see* that there was another way.

With my mind full of thoughts of Kiera, I looked ahead at the wolves that led us back to our cells, and feared that I would never see her again. I could hear the distant sound of the wolves whopping it up at the thought of mine and Jack's public execution. The sound of their bloodthirsty howls rumbled like thunder from above ground. The town of Wasp Water was full of the fucking things – the wolves had taken it over – it was their home now, and Luke Bishop was their king. He *ruled* them. Did these wolves know they were being governed by a freaking bat? I guessed not. He was known as the Wolf Man – not the Wolf Bat. But then again, anything seemed possible in this fucked up world we were now all trapped in. Ahead, I could see an open cell door and the wolves led me and Jack towards it. One of the wolves was a Skin-walker cop. He looked human enough in his starched police uniform, but a wolf lived beneath it. Whoever the poor bastard had once been, he had long ago been matched by the wolves in a school similar to that of Ravenwood. Would I have ripped his fucking head off if my hands were free – yes, I sure would. The human didn't exist anymore. His brain had been pushed flat somewhere at the back of his skull to make room for the fucked up mind of the wolf. Our other two jailers were still in their wolf forms and they sauntered ahead, their long, bushy tails swishing from side to side. One was covered in a sleek coat of brilliant white fur and the other a dull, washed-out brown. They woofed and sniffed the air as their huge bodies brushed either side of the pale green walls of the cellblock. I had been in many cellblocks as a cop and they all stank of the same thing – sweaty socks, piss, and shit. The wolves' giant heads jutted from between mighty-looking flanks and it was only in such a confined space you realised how big these fuckers truly were. I glanced sideways at Jack and again remembered how he had only minutes before ripped several of them to pieces as if they were nothing more than arse-paper.

Jack Seth stooped his bony shoulders and lowered his head as he stepped into the cell. I followed him. The cell was lit with a torch, which burned in one corner. The flames flickered, casting shadows over the stone walls. There was a bed in one corner with what looked like a urine-stained mattress. The Skin-walker in the cop uniform stood in the open cell doorway and looked at us. The other two wolves stood just behind him in the corridor.

"Don't bother to make yourselves comfortable," the Skin-walker said, eyeing us with his bright, crazy eyes. "You'll be taken above ground for your execution within the hour."

"If it's all the same to you, I'd rather we just got it over with. All this excitement is killing me," I quipped back at him.

"You'll be dead soon enough," The Skin-walker snarled, its lips rolling back to reveal its dagger-sharp teeth.

"No chance of one last meal? A cheeseburger, perhaps?" I said with a smile.

"This isn't some kind of a fucking hotel..." the Skin-walker started. Before he'd had the chance to finish, the Skin-walker shot violently forward into the cell. As if anticipating this somehow, Jack quickly stepped to one side in the narrow space. The Skin-walker's head smacked sickeningly off the cell wall and he spun around with a kind of bewildered, vacant look on his face. With the same kind of stunned expression of my own, I looked across the cell at Jack. Jack looked sideways at the open cell door. One of the wolves, the one with the brown fur, crept into the cell on his massive paws. Its long, sharp claws made a clacking sound, like high heels on the stone floor.

The Skin-walker put one hand to his forehead and wobbled like a drunk as his brain scrambled to work out exactly what had just happened. With his other hand, he fumbled for the Taser-stick that swung from his utility belt. Before he'd had the chance to release it, the wolf reared up on its back legs, opened its colossal jaws, and closed them completely over the head of the Skin-walker. My skin went cold at the sound of a muffled scream from deep within the wolf's mouth as the Skin-walker suddenly realised his fate. The Skin-walker momentarily thrashed his arms about, then stopped, just like my own heart nearly did at the cracking sound as the wolf tightened its jaws around the Skin-walker's skull. The sound of bones being crunched was deafening, and if my hands hadn't been restrained behind my back, I would have placed them over my ears. The munching and crunching was followed by a gut-wrenching slopping sound as the wolf took off the Skin-walker's head as easily as sucking a ripe cherry from its stalk. The Skin-walker's body almost seemed to stagger backwards two paces, then slide down the cell wall. The wolf worked its mighty jaws up and down as it chewed on the head now encased inside its mouth. Blood, snot, and fuck knows what else – it looked like brains – swung from the corners of the wolf's jaws as it swallowed the last of the Skin-walker's head.

I glanced back towards the open cell door to see the white fur-covered wolf step inside. With the other wolf woofing down the last of the Skin-walker's brains, the white wolf stood up on its back legs and howled. With one long claw, it made a cut from just beneath its neck and all the way down the underside of its body to its belly. Then, pulling the giant wound open in a spray of red blood and fur, the wolf seemed to step out of its very own skin to reveal a naked woman. I blinked twice, not believing what I was seeing. It was like there had been this beautiful woman standing there the whole time wearing a white fur coat and I hadn't been able to see it. Naked, she crossed the cell to the bed. She knelt, reached beneath it, and pulled out a bundle of clothes which must have been hidden there at some earlier point in time. The clothes were tied with a length of string which the female unknotted. She unravelled the clothes and pulled on a pair of blue jeans, sweater, and a long white fur coat. She tightened the coat at the waist and pulled the collar up about her neck. The woman looked at me, then at Jack. Just like the fur coat this woman wore, her thick, shoulder-length hair was just as white. Her piercing eyes twinkled yellow and her full lips were blood red.

With my heart pounding in my chest, and pulling at the chains about my wrists, I looked back at Jack, and suspecting he was a part of what had just happened, I said, "So what's with the Marilyn Monroe lookalike?"

Jack ignored me. He looked at the woman and said, "Good to see you again, Lilly Blu."

I had heard that name before. Lilly Blu was the wolf Kiera said she had to find. But more important than that, Lilly Blu had once gone by a different name. That name had been Penelope Flack. And in the world before it had been *pushed*, she had been Murphy's lover and the mother of his two daughters.

Chapter Two

Jack

I ignored Potter and looked at Lilly Blu.

"Good to see you again after so many years," I said, not surprised by her appearance, but grateful for it at least. Just like the fucking humans and Vampyrus, wolves were becoming harder and harder to trust – but I hoped I could trust her. The world was no longer the same – not because it had been *pushed* – I'd had plenty of time to come to terms with that fact – the wolves in this new world were no longer the same. There seemed to be very little loyalty between them. Had there ever been much? Not really – but there had been some, and that had been enough. So I couldn't give a shit about the Skin-walker that had just had its head bitten off. They weren't really wolves anyhow. I had never been truly happy with that part of the deal when the Wasp Water Treaty had been made. There were very few wolves left that could change into human form at will – only those that had been pushed from the other world could do that. But with the help of Bishop they had found a way – by matching with human children. It wasn't the matching that bothered me – I had killed plenty of those little fuckers throughout my time, but a wolf is a wolf, not some freaky forced mismatch, so wolves could masquerade as humans. And the process didn't always work. The Berserkers were the result of that. Bishop had never understood my unease, taking pleasure in reminding me that I too had once been human until the Elders had cursed us. He could see no difference between those like me who had once been fully human and had been cursed, and those humans who had been matched with a wolf. He blurred the lines for me until I could no longer see the difference – but there was a difference – deep inside of me, I was sure of that.

Over time, alliances change and I wasn't so sure of my allegiance to Luke Bishop anymore. Two hundred years ago we both had a common goal – a purpose that drove us – and that was waiting for the return of Kiera Hudson to this new world we had been *pushed* into. We wanted to fuck with her like she had fucked with us in The Hollows. Me and Bishop had both wanted to make her and her friends suffer and watch each of them in turn die. But I felt differently now. Not about her friends – they could die for all I cared – but not Kiera. When I had made that pact with Bishop all those years ago, I had just wanted revenge. I had been happy to make a pact with Bishop with the intention we would torment, torture, and then murder Kiera Hudson. But that plan didn't rest easy with me anymore, and that's why I couldn't let Bishop use Potter to ensnare Kiera. Bishop was still ignorant to the fact that me and Kiera were brother and sister and I needed to keep it like that – for now, at least.

When Kiera had set me free from that room as Potter and Murphy approached, I knew she couldn't let me die at the hands of those who sought me out, and I knew I could no longer lead her to Bishop. So my plans had to drastically change, but I feared I had already set too much in place – mine and Bishop's plans were too far advanced. The photographer had already changed much, and I didn't know if there was any way of unravelling that. So I had sent out the only wolf I still trusted with a message that I needed to speak with Lilly Blu. We had met only once before – many years ago – but she was known to have an understanding of the layers – the different *whens* and *wheres.* Where her knowledge came from, I didn't know or care. That was her business – but she had an understanding, and that was enough for me. If anyone could seal the cracks that the photographer had created, then it was Lilly Blu. The one thing I knew for certain was she had very little love for Bishop and the Treaty. I didn't know whether the photographer was a friend or foe, let alone the photographer's identity. All I knew was that this photographer had an understanding of the *wheres* and *whens* just like Lilly Blu did.

But would Lilly help me? I couldn't be sure. But she was here now, wasn't she? The wolf I had sent with the message had reached her. I broke Lilly Blu's piercing yellow stare and looked at the other wolf. Just like Lilly had, the wolf stood up on its back legs and peeled back its skin of fur like a coat. But unlike Lilly, the other let their skin fall away so it formed a pile of bloody flesh and fur on the cell floor. The wolf stood naked before us in his human form.

"Thank you, little brother," I said, looking across the cell at Nik.

"We don't have a lot of time," he said, coming behind me and breaking my chains with his powerful claws. They clattered to the floor and I rubbed my wrists with my long skeletal fingers.

"I fucking knew it," Potter said, looking at Nik. "I knew I'd seen you before. In that hangar on the outskirts of Wasp Water…"

"Where you murdered Eloisa," Nik barked back at him.

Potter shrugged his broad shoulders as if her death had meant nothing to him and said, "She had been the murderer."

"She had been like a mother to me," Nik said, closing the gap between him and Potter.

"Well I wouldn't get yourself too upset about it," Potter said, fixing Nik with his black eyes. "People have a habit of showing up here."

"We've searched for years," Nik said with a shake of his head. "Eloisa hasn't come through."

With another shrug of his shoulders, Potter said, "Well I guess that means a whole bunch of kids can sleep safely in their beds tonight. Now take off these chains, I need a smoke."

"I've got a good mind to rip your heart out, just like you did Eloisa's," Nik howled, nose to nose with Potter.

"Oh, please don't," Potter smirked. "It's only just started beating again and…"

"Kill him if you want, little brother," I said, anger beginning to swell inside of me. I hadn't wanted Potter's death to be public, so as not to draw Kiera out into the open. What happened to him deep within these cells, I really couldn't give a fuck.

Snarling, Nik raised his claws, ready to take Potter's head off.

"Stop!" Lilly Blu suddenly spoke up. "If you want to stop the photographer, then you're going to need his help."

I looked sideways at Lilly.

"We only need a drop of his blood for what I have planned," Nik told her, not taking his eyes from Potter.

"Your plans aren't my plans, and I'm telling you we need him," Lilly said, her voice soft but firm.

With his claw still raised just an inch from Potter's throat, Nik continued to stare brightly at him.

"I'd listen to the lady if I were you," Potter smiled again.

There was a moment's silence in which I half expected Nik to still rip Potter's throat out. Then, swallowing hard like I had a throat full of poison, I stepped forward and placed my hand on Nik's bare shoulder and said, "Leave him be, little brother. Another time will come when you can have revenge for what he did to Eloisa."

Slowly, I felt the muscles in Nik's shoulders loosen as he lowered his claw. He turned his head towards me, his blue eyes blazing, then sunk his fist into Potter's chest.

Chapter Three

Potter

I felt Nik's claws sink into my chest an inch, then stop. The pain was a killer and I cried out, throwing my head back and clenching my fists. I wrestled with the chains that bound my wrists, but they were too thick to be broken. I clenched my teeth as Nik opened and closed his fingers beneath my flesh. My heart thumped in my chest and this was the first time I'd felt true pain since coming into this *pushed* world. The kick-in that the Skin-walkers had given me in the snow outside the barn had hurt, but the pain had been dull compared to this. Nik's fingers felt like four red-hot pokers being driven into me.

"Fuck you," I hissed through clenched teeth.

Then, just when I thought I could take no more and the world began to swim before my eyes, Nik withdrew his fingers. They slid from out of my chest, glistening black with my blood.

"You evil sonofabitch," I groaned in pain.

Ignoring me, Nik turned to look at his brother, Jack. Through eyes as narrow as slits, I watched warm streams of my blood trickle down Nik's fingers, over his wrist, and down the length of his forearm.

I dropped my head and looked at the four black puncture wounds in the centre of my chest. The blood had already started to clot there in crimson scabs.

"Are you fucking deaf?" I spat, looking back up at Nik. "The Marilyn Monroe wannabe said you weren't to kill me."

"You're not dead, are you?" Nik said, without turning back to look at me.

"No, but you fucking will be the moment these chains are taken off," I grimaced, the pain in my chest easing with every passing moment. "I'll be sticking four of my fingers into you, and I can promise you now, I won't be aiming for your fucking chest!"

"Shut up!" the three of them suddenly barked.

"Jesuz!" Jack snarled at me. "Can't you quit your bitching for just one minute?"

"Who's bitching?" I shot back.

"Just be quiet," Jack snapped, taking a step towards me. "It's quite simple. Just keep your mouth shut. It's not like I'm asking you to fart gold or anything. Now be quiet – or do you want to go to the guillotine?"

"Anything's got to be better than..." I started.

Before I'd the chance to finish, Jack had unknotted the red bandanna from around his scrawny throat, rolled it into a ball, and stuffed it into my mouth. My eyes bulged in their sockets as I drew air up into my nostrils. Jack's bandanna was salty tasting where for years it had soaked up his sweat. I gagged as hot bile shot up into my throat.

"Quiet at last," Jack said with a sneer, turning his long narrow back on me to face his brother again.

I glanced at Lilly, but she looked away too and at Nik. Slowly, the younger wolf pushed his blood-covered fingers into his mouth and sucked my blood from them. He shot forward, and at first I thought he had rammed his fingers too far down the back of his throat and was now vomiting. I knew the feeling. But Nik wasn't sick. He pulled his fingers from his mouth and buckled forward at the waist. He cried out and dropped to his knees. Trying to work the bandanna free from my mouth with my tongue, I watched as Nik shook violently as if throwing some kind of fit. I couldn't see his face, as it was cast down towards the floor, but all the same I knew he was somehow changing. I watched in silence as his fair hair grew short and darker in colour. His thin frame began to fill out, his shoulders growing broader, his neck thicker, thighs firmer. He cried out again, as if in pain, lifting his head so as to look at me. It was then I was thankful Jack had stuffed his bandanna into my mouth, for I fear I might have screamed. To look at Nik was like looking into a mirror. He was me – he had become my identical twin. He tried to stand up and staggered backwards into the cell wall. Jack and Lilly reached for him. Taking him by the arms, they helped him to stand. Nik stood just feet away from me.

21

I looked back at myself and again I wanted to scream. Not with fear, but with madness. And it was at that moment I understood how Isidor had felt when looking at those copies of himself floating in those tanks beneath the hangar just outside of Wasp Water. Isidor had felt anger at how someone had tried to copy him, and I just hadn't understood his feelings. But as Nik came towards me, an identical replica of myself, I felt the urge to freak out, to run away as far as I could. I knew some Lycanthrope had the ability to take on the form of another by consuming their blood. Jack had copied McCain at Ravenwood, but I had never seen it happen, and never thought I would be copied. I didn't like seeing another me. And besides, surely my nose couldn't look that bent and twisted out of shape. Could it?

"Don't look so scared, Potter," Nik said, looking straight at me.

Jesus, he even sounds like me, I thought.

He reached for my face, and I flinched backwards, unable to stop looking at myself.

"I'm not going to hurt you," he said, slowly pulling the cloth from my mouth.

I gasped in a lungful of air. "What the fuck is going on here?" I muttered.

"You want to escape, don't you?" he said, looking at me.

It was like having a conversation with myself.

Before I had the chance to answer, Jack gripped Nik's shoulder and spun him around.

"No!" he barked. "I won't let you do it."

"It's the only way if you are to get out of Wasp Water and save Kiera," Nik said. "She's my sister, too, remember. I saved her once before from the zoo but I had no idea back then – in that world – who she really was. I'd like to help her again."

"There has to be another way," Jack said, realising what it was that his younger brother was suggesting.

Now I'm as smart as the next guy, and I don't know if it had something to do with the shock of seeing Nik change into me, but I didn't have a fucking clue as to what was going on.

Then as if in answer to my own questions, Jack said to Nik, "I won't let you take Potter's place beneath the guillotine."

"There isn't any other way," Nik said as I watched them. "Luke has to believe – the world has to believe – that both you and Potter are dead. If they think you have simply escaped, they will come looking for you – they will hunt you down."

To look at them was like having some kind of out-of-body experience as I watched myself deep in conversation with Jack Seth.

"Nik is right," Lilly said, looking up into Jack's wizened face. "If Luke believes you are both dead, it will give us the breathing space we need to try and unmask this photographer."

"You don't know who it is?" Jack glanced at her.

"No," she said with a shake of her thick head of white hair.

Jack looked at the both of them and said, "I won't let my younger brother pay the price for a crime he didn't commit."

"But you did the same for me, before the world got pushed," Nik reminded him. "You let Potter and the others believe it was you who murdered all of those young women, but it was me. You went on trial before the Elders to protect me."

"I was given twelve life sentences, not the death sentence," Jack reminded him.

"For a wolf to be imprisoned deep within The Hollows amongst those Vampyrus is worse than death, and you know it," Nik said, looking and sounding exactly like me.

"But there was always a chance of escape," Jack said.

"I've escaped death once before, Jack," Nik said. "Perhaps I can do it again."

"Then let Potter take that chance," Jack said, as if I were no longer present in the cell. Then looking at Lilly, Jack added, "Is there an escape for my brother if he does this? You understand the *wheres* and *whens* better than anyone."

"There is no coming back – not to this when," Lilly said, shaking her head. "Maybe not to any *when,* not ever again."

"Did you hear what she said?" Jack said, turning on his younger brother. "I won't let you take Potter's place."

23

"I don't need anyone to stand in for me," I said, hooking a piece of red thread from between my teeth with my little finger. "I ain't no coward."

"It's not about who has the biggest set of balls," Lilly said, glaring at me. "It's who serves more purpose here – in this when."

"Well if you speak to most of the people who know me, they'd tell you I served no fucking purpose at all, so I guess it's me who should go to the guillotine," I said, keeping one eye on my lookalike.

"I want to do this," Nik said, looking back at his brother.

"But why?" Jack demanded. "You're my brother."

"And Kiera is our sister," Nik reminded him. "We've already had two lifetimes together, it's time you shared one with Kiera."

"What makes you so sure that I want to?" Jack growled at him.

"Because you haven't led her to Luke Bishop like you were meant to," Nik said. "Jack, apart from me, you've never helped anyone in your life. She must mean something to you as you're facing the guillotine because of her."

Jack lowered his head, then said without looking at his brother, "I can't choose between my brother and sister."

"Nobody is asking you to choose," Nik said. "It's my choice. I want to do this for you and Kiera, Jack. I was lucky enough to have spent time with Kiera in that zoo, and I wish I had known then that she was my sister. But you know what? In a way I'm glad I didn't know back in that world. If I'd known, I might only have helped her because of that fact. But in my heart I know I helped Kiera because she was worth helping – she was worth saving, Jack. And she's worth saving now. But this time, it's your chance to save her."

I watched silently as Jack raised his head and looked at his brother. Even though Nik now looked identical to me, Jack slowly drew one bony thumb down the side of his brother's face.

"Thank you, Nikolaou," Jack whispered.

Feeling as if I should say something too, after all, the wolf was saving my arse, I said, "Yeah, thanks Niko-whatever-your-name-is."

"I'm not doing it for you," Nik barked back at me.

"Sure," I said, biting my tongue so I wouldn't make some cocky comeback.

From deep within the cellblock, the silence was suddenly broken by the rattle of keys.

"They're coming for you," Nik said, pushing his brother towards the open cell door. "Go!"

Lilly crossed the cell, came up behind me, and swiped away the chains which bound me. They clattered to the floor. "We've got to get moving," she breathed in my ear.

I headed towards the cell door, then looked back. "No offence or anything, and I don't want to piss all over your plan," I said, "but I get the whole creepy lookalike thing with me, the wolves are gonna think they are executing me when really it is you, but what about Jack? Aren't they gonna wonder where he's disappeared to?"

Without saying anything, Nik bent down and covered his hands and forearms in the flesh and fur that he had cast aside when removing his wolf skin. With his hands and arms bright red with flesh and blood, he smeared some across his chin. Then, standing and looking at me, he said, "Knowing that death was near, and unable to control your hatred for the wolves, you killed and then ate your cellmate, Jack Seth, as your last supper."

"Nice," I said, furrowing my brow. "You sure got it all figured out."

"There is nothing more cunning than a wolf," Nik said, staring back at me.

"That's for sure," I said, turning my back on him and leaving the cell.

Chapter Four

Jack

I waited for Lilly and Potter to leave the cell. The sound of approaching cops was ringing louder in my ears with every passing moment. Still I stopped at the door and looked at my brother. He sat on the bed, looking identical to the man I'd spent most of my adult life hating and wanting to kill. But under that skin, I knew it was Nik who sat there waiting to take my enemy's place beneath the guillotine. He looked up at me and stared through Potter's dead black eyes.

"You don't have to do this," I told him, swallowing the lump that had suddenly appeared in my throat.

"Yes, I do," he said, sounding just like that dick Potter.

"But..."

"Jack, they're coming, and if they catch you here then we will all die and all of this would've been for nothing," he said.

I looked down at the torn pieces of flesh and fur that covered the cell floor, knowing that Luke and his merry band of Skinwalkers would believe it to be me – killed by Potter – my brother – before being taken to his death. The sound of heavy footfalls grew closer still, the *thud-thud-thud* of them echoing off the stone corridor walls of the custody block.

"Run, Jack!" Nik whispered.

I looked back at the cell door, then again at my brother. Reaching out with one long skinny hand, I ran my fingers through his short black hair. It didn't feel like my brother's hair and nor did it look like it. I closed my eyes and pictured Nik as a small boy, sitting on the rug before the fire at our mother's house, as he played with his toy cars. I could see the light from the fire reflecting back in his almost white-blond hair and in his pale blue eyes. That was Nik – that was my little brother I could see, before like me, he turned into a killer – an animal.

"I love you, brother," I whispered with my eyes closed.

With them still squeezed shut, I turned, so I didn't have to see him sitting on that bed looking like Potter. I didn't want to remember him like that. I stepped into the corridor outside the cell. I opened my eyes, and without looking back, I closed the cell door on my brother. I looked to the right, and could see Lilly and Potter hiding in the shadows further along the cellblock. I headed towards them. With my eyes fixed on Potter, I headed straight for him. Curling my bony fingers into a fist, I punched him squarely in the face. There was a cracking sound as my fist crunched into the flat of his nose and he shot back down the corridor, landing on the floor.

"What the fuck was that for?" he gargled as his nose and mouth filled with blood.

"It made me feel better," I grunted, walking on past him and into the shadows at the end of the corridor.

"No wonder my fucking nose looks the way it does," I heard him mutter, pulling himself to his feet. "What, with Murphy's driving and people queuing up to take pot-shots at me the whole fucking time..."

"Maybe you shouldn't be such a prick, and perhaps people wouldn't feel the need to slap you so much," I said over my shoulder at him.

"Who are you calling a prick...?" Potter started.

"Give me a break," Lilly said, brushing past me and heading up the corridor. "We're meant to be escaping! Save your differences until we're out of here."

I followed Lilly without saying another word, Potter moaning and groaning, puffing and panting behind us as he tried to stem the flow of blood gushing from his nose. I smiled to myself in the darkness, as Lilly rounded a bend in the corridor ahead. She led us into a narrow passageway. There was a gated door at the end, and weak streams of light poured in through the bars and lit the corridor. We headed towards the light.

I watched as Lilly fished a key from the pocket of her white fur coat. She slipped the key into a rusty-looking lock, and yanked the gate open. We spilled out into the light to find ourselves standing on what once must have been the exercise yard. The concrete was cracked and weeds grew tall out of them. The white markings of a basketball court were now almost faded away. Much of the fencing and razor wire had come down in places, and what was left was orange-brown with rust. Beyond the fence I could see what looked like a piece of scrubland which led away to a more overgrown and hilly area.

"Follow me," Lilly ordered, edging her way along the side of the cellblock and towards an opening in what was once the fence. I looked back to see Potter stagger out into the light. Thick clots of black blood had already formed around his nostrils. His coat flapped open and I could see that the wounds Nik had made on his chest had now healed completely. There was no sign of them.

Those Vampyrus fuckers heal quickly, I thought, inching my way along the outside of the jail wall. *No wonder you have to take their heads off if you want to kill them.*

Potter scowled at me, then followed us along the wall. I could hear the sound of chanting coming from the main town square and I knew the wolves were getting excited for the execution. I had been to many myself and enjoyed each of them. But today it was going to be my brother they were executing. I tried to block out the sounds of the howling and whooping of the excited wolves in the town square.

Lilly hunkered down as we reached the hole in the fence. She looked back at us and said, "Head for the hill."

Pulling back the rusty fence with her slender fingers, Lilly crawled through the hole and raced across the scrubland, disappearing behind some bushes in the distance. I followed, Potter at my heels. Reaching the bushes, I lay flat on the ground in the dust. Potter lay beside me. I didn't look at him for fear of wanting to smash him in the face again. There was an ear-piercing wail from somewhere in the distance.

"What was that?" Potter whispered. "Is that an alarm or something?"

"It's the DJ switching on his microphone," I whispered from the corner of my mouth.

"DJ?" Potter breathed. "I thought they had gathered for an execution – not a freaking party!"

"The party comes after," I said, still unable to bring myself to look at him.

"Fucking wolves," Potter grunted.

Before I'd had the chance to point out the many Vampyrus faults, the voice of the DJ, who whipped up the crowd, bellowed out through the speakers erected in the town of Wasp Water.

"Welcome to today's executions," the voice echoed across the town. "Do we have a surprise for you all today!"

The crowd roared in the distance, their cheers of excitement sounding like an approaching storm. I knew at this point they would be shoving and pushing against each other to get as close to the stage as possible. I had been in there with them so many times before, and I couldn't deny that it was fucking exciting. It was like the whole town square was charged with electricity. I knew each of the wolves would want the best possible view. To look into the eyes of the accused as the blade came down – there was nothing more exciting than that. To see that realisation in the human's eyes as they heard the screech and the scrape of the blade racing down towards their necks. The look of fear in their eyes would drive me insane with excitement. But it was more than excitement – that word didn't do justice to how seeing a human die made me feel. It was a turn on – it was like having an orgasm that lasted all night long.

"Are you all right?" I heard someone whisper.

"Huh?" I said, glancing sideways and looking into Potter's ugly face.

"You have a crazy kinda look on your face," he said, staring at me with a frown from beneath the blood smeared over his face. "You look like you're gonna come in your pants or something. That is your brother they're gonna kill anytime now…"

"I don't need you to remind me my brother is going to die today," I hissed through gritted teeth at him. "I was just remembering…"

"Remembering what?" Potter said, still looking confused. "The first time you beat yourself off?"

"Fuck you, Potter," I spat, crawling away on my belly. I just wanted to be away from him. I didn't need him judging me. I knew he enjoyed killing as much as I did. That was the problem with the Vampyrus – they refused to admit that their shit stank just as bad as the wolves' did.

"No, fuck you," Potter said, coming after me on his knees. "You were getting off on the thought of there being an execution, you twisted sonofabitch."

When I knew I was out of sight from the jail and hidden behind some trees, I scrambled to my feet and rounded on Potter. Before I'd had a chance to reach for him, he too had sprung to his feet.

"Okay, so let's not delay the main event any longer!" the DJ yelled through the speaker. His high-pitched voice echoed back off the surrounding hills. "Please welcome to the stage, our executioner!"

I could hear the crowd erupt in a chorus of cheers and whistles. I knew the executioner in his black hood would now be stepping out onto the stage.

"Do you like the sound of that?" Potter barked at me, pointing back towards the town. "Is that how you get your kicks?"

"Don't you dare judge me," I barked, going toe-to-toe with Potter. I towered over him, but he refused to budge.

"Kill him! Kill him! Kill him!" the wolves chanted in the distance and for a moment I thought they were urging me on to rip Potter's head off. I clenched my fists, digging my nails into the balls of my hands instead of Potter's upturned face. The desire to kill him once and for all was overwhelming.

Then just as I thought I wouldn't be able to stop myself from killing him, Lilly shoved herself between us.

"It's like being with a couple of kids. How are you two ever going to save Kiera Hudson if you can't even talk to each other without getting into a fight?"

"He started it," Potter said. "He punched me in the goddamn face!"

"You want to be thankful I didn't…" I started, his whining starting to piss me off again.

"Please, can you both stop bitching for just one minute?" Lilly sighed with frustration, placing her hands on her hips. She stared at the both of us with her bright eyes. "You two are giving me a freaking headache. Now both apologise to each other and make up or…"

"Oh this is just fucking great," Potter laughed, crusty dried blood flaking away from beneath his nose and around the corners of his mouth. "If you honestly believe that I'm gonna say sorry, then you're crazier than him, sweetheart."

Lilly glared at me and said, "Say sorry, Jack."

"Yeah, say sorry, Jack," Potter cut in.

"No!" I howled. "Never!"

"See," Potter said, looking at Lilly. "The guy's a freaking idiot."

"And so are you!" Lilly shouted, prodding Potter in the chest with one bright red fingernail. "Even though you both know that the woman you both claim to love is in mortal danger – you still can't bury your differences to help her. Well, if you two can't be bothered, then why should I be? It looks like I've wasted my time in coming here. I should have let both of you die."

I watched Lilly storm away, her long, white fur coat flapping about her heels as she marched up the side of the hill. I glanced at Potter, then back at Lilly's retreating figure. Turning my back on Potter, I followed her up the hillside.

Chapter Five

Potter

If Lilly Blu honestly thought Jack Seth would ever get an apology from me, then she better head straight back to the crack den she'd obviously come from. She must be off her freaking head if she thought I'd ever say sorry to that streaky piece of shit. I would never say sorry to any wolf, regardless if they saved my life or not. They were all child-murdering scum as far as I was concerned. I saw the look in that freak's eyes as he heard the wolves cheering at the thought of an execution. The thought of it was getting him excited. That was his little brother they were gonna kill, for fuck's sake.

I watched Jack turn away and head up the hill after Lilly Blu. Apart from her obvious beauty, God only knows what Murphy ever saw in her.

"And he always accused me of thinking with my dick," I muttered to myself, heading up the hill after Jack and Lilly. It was almost impossible to breathe as my nose was clogged with dry clots of blood. I pushed my forefinger into my right nostril and hooked out one of the scabs of dry blood. Rolling it into a ball between my thumb and forefinger, I flicked it at Jack's back.

"Have some of that, you fucking pervert," I muttered.

It stuck to the back of his blue denim shirt.

"Did you say something?" Jack sneered over his shoulder at me.

"Nope," I shrugged. "It must be your delusional other self you can hear. Maybe it's your conscience talking."

Jack made a huffing noise, and faced front again. I picked a piece of flaky dried blood from my top lip and flicked this at Jack's back. This time my aim wasn't so great, and it pinged off the back of his neck. Jack slapped the back of his neck with his hand as if swatting a gnat. Seeing this, I laughed.

"What the fuck is wrong with you?" Jack glared back again at me. This time he stopped, so he could turn and face me.

"It's nothing," I said, trying to stifle my laughter.

"So you often burst into uncontrollable fits of laughter for no reason?" Jack spat. "And here I was thinking I was the only one with problems."

"There's no problem," I glared at him.

Not liking being laughed at, Jack strode down the hill towards me.

"Tell me what's so freaking funny, Potter, or I'll rip your..." Jack suddenly stopped as if something had caught his attention from over my shoulder.

I turned around to see what it was that had grabbed his attention. From our position high up on the side of the hill, the town of Wasp Water lay sprawled below us. We had a bird's eye view of the town square and the wolves pressed into it. I could see the stage that had been erected. The sounds of their cheering and chanting swept towards us on the wind.

"UNMASK HIM! UNMASK HIM! UNMASK HIM!" The wolves howled below.

I could see the executioner standing behind a hooded figure. That figure didn't need to be unmasked for me to know who was beneath it. The guy with the microphone pressed to his lips stepped forward, and yanked off the prisoner's hood. Again, I had that unnerving feeling of experiencing some kind of out-of-body experience as I watched myself being unmasked in the town square. I had to remind myself that it wasn't me or a twin – it was Nik who had taken my place so that I could be free to help Kiera and my friends. Then turning cold, I spotted Kiera desperately fighting to reach the stage. Not to get a better view of the impending execution, but to try and save the man she loved – *me*. My new heart ached as I saw her throw her hands to her face and cry out at the sight of me on the stage. My face – Nik's face – was swollen and bruised. Those who had come to the cell to collect him had obviously beaten him when discovering the remains of what they believed to be Jack Seth. Nik's eyes were swollen shut and my already bent out of shape nose was spread across my face like a flattened tomato.

"KILL HIM!" the crowd cried.

I watched as Kiera fought her way through the crowd and towards the stage. I took a step forward on the hillside wanting to go to her. To tell her that it wasn't really me they were going to kill. I was desperate to let her know that Nik had swapped places with me. I took another step forward, then felt a hand fall on my shoulder.

"No," Jack whispered, "or my brother's death would be for nothing."

With my heart pounding in my chest, I looked down into the town square again.

The wolves appeared to be throwing objects at the stage. These objects bounced off Nik, staining his naked upper torso red and black.

"What are they throwing?" I asked, feeling numb at the sight of such brutality.

"Human remains," Jack whispered, and I thought that perhaps I detected just the faintest note of shame in his voice.

I didn't say anything. What was there to say? Words seemed so inadequate as I stood and watched Nik being forced down over the guillotine. I watched him lower his head as if accepting his fate. That should have been me – not him. That was my fate – right or wrong – that should have been *me*. I stepped forward again, a sudden urge to take the young wolf's place.

Another hand gripped my left forearm.

"No," a voice whispered. I glanced left to see Lilly standing beside me. The wind tugged her white hair from around her face, revealing her striking beauty. I looked back down at the town square, and could see Kiera push her way towards the stage. Nik still had his head cast down.

The wolves continued to roar and howl. I could see the pain on Kiera's face as she fought desperately to reach me. I just wanted to go to her, to hold her in my arms and tell her that I was safe. Sensing that I might bolt free at any moment, I felt both Lilly and Jack tighten their grips on me.

"We have to stop this," I said. "We can't let Nik die and we can't let Kiera believe I'm dead. It's wrong."

"Try and stop it now and we're all dead," Lilly said, matter-of-factly. "What good would that do?"

"But that's your brother down there," I said, looking at Jack.

"And so is my sister," he said back, his face gaunt and taut-looking. There was no fire in his eyes now. "If we can put things right – maybe *push* back a little – then my brother's death wouldn't have been for nothing."

I looked back at the town square to see the blade of the guillotine come racing down, the winter sunlight winking back at me from its razor-sharp edge. The crowd roared with excitement. I felt Jack's hand slide slowly from my shoulder as he turned his narrow back on the scene below. I watched as Kiera reached for me, then buckle to her knees. The crowd of wolves seemed to wash over her like a wave.

"Kiera!" I cried out.

"Shhh!" Lilly warned me, pulling at my arm, dragging me back up the hill.

"Get the fuck off me," I growled, pushing her hand from me. I peered back down into the square. I desperately scanned the crowds for any sign of Kiera. "I've got to help her."

"No!" Lilly howled.

"But..." I started.

"Potter, c'mon," Lilly almost seemed to plead, yanking at the sleeve of my coat again.

Then I saw another face I recognised in the crowd. It was Meren, and Kiera was with her. Meren was leading Kiera back through the crowd, out of town, and away from danger. I lost sight of them behind a row of houses. I ran back up the hill to get a better view. I ran frantically up and down between the trees in search of a glimpse of Kiera and Meren. I had to know that Kiera got away safely.

"There's Kiera!" I gasped, pointing down onto the road that led out of town.

"We should get going," Lilly said. "It's not safe here."

From high up on the hillside, I looked down at Meren, her arm wrapped around Kiera as she led her out of Wasp Water. It was then I remembered the connection between Meren and Lilly. Meren was Lilly's daughter.

"C'mon," Lilly hissed, yanking at my arm again.

Glancing back at her, I said, "I can't leave Kiera as quickly as you were prepared to leave your..." I stopped myself before I said any more.

"What were you going to say?" Lilly asked, staring at me, the collar of her white fur coat flapping about the sides of her face.

"Nothing," I whispered, looking away and back at the road. I couldn't tell Lilly that the girl helping Kiera out of Wasp Water was her daughter. Was Lilly the same Lilly who Murphy had loved when she had called herself Penelope Flack? That had been in a different *when* and *where*. Did she remember that life, or had she forgotten about Murphy and her daughters, just like Sophie Harrison had forgotten all about me? Remembering me had only caused Sophie a world of pain and ultimately her death, so I decided not to say anything to Lilly about Meren.

I watched as Kiera dropped to her knees on the road just outside of town, and again, I had to fight the overwhelming urge to go to her.

"Kiera is safely out of town," Jack said, coming up beside me and looking down at the road.

"Then we can go to her," I said. "We can tell her that I'm still alive."

"No," Lilly said. "Kiera has to believe that you're dead if you and Jack are going to *push* back!"

Chapter Six

Jack

Lilly led us away from the side of the hill. The cheers and roar of the hungry crowd in the square eventually faded like a dream on waking. Potter dragged behind. I didn't look back often, but when I did, he too was looking back in the direction we had come. I knew he was thinking about Kiera. He had struggled to walk away and leave her out on the road, broken and crying. I had to tell myself that I was doing a good thing by walking away and following Lilly over the hill and down into the valley on the other side. But who was I trying to kid? I'd forgotten how to be good a whole lifetime ago. Being *good* didn't come easy to me. I struggled with that. I rubbed my right temple with my fingers, then loosened the bandana about my throat. Sometimes the thoughts of killing gnawed away at me. It was like they hacked away at my brains like an ice-pick. When the urge to kill was bad, it felt like I was being strangled by my desires. It was an addiction that I had struggled with my whole life. I rubbed my temples again as the sun began to set in the west like an eye swollen with blood. Was addiction the right word? An addiction could be beat – it could be broken – so why couldn't I stop killing? My first kill had been my own mother and that had been the sweetest. To kill the person who had brought so much pain to my life had felt like more than just revenge. It had given me the taste – the hunger to kill again. I had murdered so many women and children now, that I had lost count of the number of my victims – but one thing I had never forgotten was how the first had felt so fucking good. I had never managed to recapture that high again. I had tried, believe me. Yes, sir. I'd tried to spice my killings up a bit by adding some torture into the mix – even some fucking amputations – but nothing had been quite like my first. Had the first kill felt so good because it had been my mother? I didn't know. But one thing was for sure – I'd searched for that feeling my whole life but had never been able to recapture it. Eloisa had helped me with my cravings.

She had taught me the pleasures of new highs of a different kind. We had sex often. Eloisa's appetite and willingness to please had been unmatchable. She had been a monster in her own way. I hadn't killed once during my time with Eloisa – I had discovered a different kind of satisfaction. But when she had gone – murdered by Potter – it didn't take me long to fall back into my old ways. But this time it was worse for me. I had two cravings to satisfy and when they were bought together – the trip I got was truly mind-fucking-blowing. Even that Hen Party of human females I'd worked my way through in that hotel room did little to sedate my murderous desires. Even though I left that hotel room looking something close to a fucking slaughterhouse, I still wanted more. The way in which I had defiled their bodies hadn't been enough. The cops were still looking for the sonofabitch who raped and slaughtered those seventeen young women, even though it had happened over thirty-five years ago. I doubted they would ever stop looking. I'd killed plenty more since then – but that had been me at my worst – or *best* – I sometimes thought with a smile. But still it had not given me the rush of my first kill. Nothing had come close to that. Would I ever feel such intensity in my soul again? I doubted it, and there was a part of me that really didn't give a shit anymore. Something was changing deep within me. It had started in that room with Kiera. I'd ensnared her there to kill her – perhaps killing my sister would've given me the orgasmic thrill I'd been searching for. But something happened. I don't know what – I can't put my finger on it – but there was something. I started to change in that room. I'd thought about it ever since. I hadn't been able to sleep. Each long and drawn out night I had spent trying to figure out what it was she had done to me in that room. Had she tricked me in some way? Cast a spell over me perhaps? No, she had done neither of those things. But I had started to feel something I hadn't since...

"I recognise this place," a voice said, cutting into my private thoughts.

I looked up to find myself standing outside what looked like a disused railway station. As if I had been on autopilot, I had blindly followed Lilly into a deserted town. I glanced back over my shoulder and could see that Potter had come to halt a few feet behind me. It was dark now, and the sun had fully set while I had been lost in thought. We stood in a wide road. The pavement was so cracked with age that it looked like someone had covered the road in slabs of crazy paving. The buildings which lined the streets appeared semi demolished, as if the town had been involved in some kind of military conflict. Much of what was left was little more than burnt-out rubble. Cars, which were no more than empty shells, lay on their sides or upside down in the street. The seats had been ripped out, as had the dashboards and steering wheels. Weeds and other wild plant life now covered much of their sun-bleached and rusty frames. I looked to my right, and further down the street I could see a traffic signal blinking off and on like a red eye.

Remembering what Potter had said, I looked back at him and said, "You've been here before?"

"Not exactly," Potter said, looking at the railway station set a little way back from the derelict looking street. He took a crumpled pack of cigarettes from his pocket and popped one into the corner of his mouth.

"What's that s'posed to mean?" I asked.

"This station looks kinda familiar, but it was someplace else before," Potter said, blowing smoke through his nostrils. "The last time I saw a station like this, it was in a valley... it was where Isidor died..."

"Hey, where is this place?" I asked Lilly, losing patience with whatever it was Potter was blathering on about.

"Nowhere," Lilly said with a shrug of her shoulders while approaching the front of the station.

"No, I'm mistaken," Potter said with a shake of his head as if waking from a dream. "It's not the same station. This one is far bigger. Far grander than I first thought."

"What are you talking about?" I barked, looking at him. "This place is a poky little shithole."

"Is it?" I heard Lilly say.

I turned to look at her to discover that she was standing halfway up a set of grey stone steps which led to the front of the grandest railway station I had ever seen. At the top of the steps stood four stone pillars. Set between these were huge wooden doors which would have been more suited fixed into the front of a cathedral. Over the doors and engraved into the white stone above them were the words *The Great Western Railway.*

I looked back over my shoulder and the street looked just as it had before, with its overturned cars, demolished buildings, and cracked paving stones.

"The station didn't look like this just a minute ago..." I breathed, turning to face Lilly again.

She was now standing on the very top step. Her long, white fur coat flapped silently about her long legs in the breeze. "It's always looked like this, Jack." She smiled down at me. "The darkness must be playing tricks on you."

It was night alright, but what little moonlight shone from behind the clouds still told me that she was wrong, the station had looked like little more than a dilapidated hut with a rickety wooden platform just moments ago. Even Potter had thought it had reminded him of someplace else. I glanced sideways at him to discover that Potter was now halfway up the steps and heading towards Lilly at the top.

Chapter Seven

Potter

I joined Lilly on the top step. Some crazy shit was taking place here and it made me feel uneasy. The station had at first looked like that little station set in that deep valley as me and my friends had fled the Berserkers. It had looked just like the place Isidor had died in that ancient-looking waiting room. But then it hadn't looked like that place at all. The station now looked like the mother of all fucking railway stations. And how had we gotten here? We hadn't been walking too long. How had Lilly led us over that hill and into this ramshackle of a town? I wasn't aware of such a big town being so close to Wasp Water. But then again, there could be in this new, screwed up world we had been brought back to. From the top of the steps I looked back at the town. It was nothing more than a mass of gutted buildings and derelict streets. The town was eerily quiet and the only thing I could hear was Lilly's coat flapping about her heels. Jack started up the steps towards us, his long, spidery legs casting stretched shadows in the moonlight.

"Where is this place?" I asked Lilly, shooting her a sideways glance.

"It's a railway station," she smiled with her full red lips.

Christ, she looked like Marilyn Monroe, I thought, watching how her thick white-blonde hair curled about her shoulders. Why did female wolves have to be so freaking hot? I pushed those thoughts from my head and said, "I asked *where* this place is, not *what* it is. I can see it's a freaking railway station."

"It's *nowhere*," she said with a knowing smile.

"What sort of a bullshit answer is that?" I groaned.

Jack joined us on the top step.

"The Great Western Railway, it says above the door," he said, looking down at Lilly. "It looks more like Grand Central Station."

I looked up at the lettering engraved into the white stonework above the giant doors. "I saw Grand Central Station in

41

a movie once... before I died, that is... and you know, you might be right for once, Jack, this place looks a lot like that station, but we sure as hell are not in New..."

A high-pitched wailing noise, like fingernails being scraped down a chalkboard, drowned out my last word. I looked away from the sign to discover Lilly was pushing open one of the giant doors. I looked at Jack, who stared back at me. Then, together, we followed Lilly into the station. The door swung shut behind us with a boom. I looked back and it had gone. There was no doorway. Where the door had been was now just more of the same grey stone wall and a billboard poster which read: "Holidays aboard the Scorpion Steam. There is no other way to travel!" Beneath the writing on the poster was a picture of a huge black steam train. Clouds of thick grey smoke billowed out of its funnel and the cow catcher at the front of the train was as black as coal. It was wide and pointed, giving the steam train the appearance of having a malevolent grin.

"Where's the door gone?" I asked, turning my back on the wall and the poster.

"Jeez," I heard Jack hiss through his broken front teeth.

I followed his stare and looked out across the railway station. It was huge – cavernous. Unlike the desolate and demolished streets outside, the main concourse thrived with people. They bustled back and forth. As I looked closer, I could see that some of these people were wandering around looking lost, as if caught in a dream. Others strode across the polished concourse with purpose, as if they knew exactly where they were going.

"Follow me," Lilly said, thrusting her hands into the pockets of her fur coat.

Without saying a word, Jack and I followed Lilly across the concourse. About halfway across, we came to a wooden bench. Lilly sat down.

"Sit," she whispered with a smile.

We sat on either side of her on the bench.

"I love to people watch," she whispered again as if frightened she might disturb those that wandered around the station. "Watch... listen."

Sitting on the bench, I could hear the sound of train guards blowing whistles. I could hear the *clackety-clack* of trains passing over tracks and points.

"I can hear trains – lots of trains, but can't see any," I breathed.

"There are platforms with trains but you have to go below ground to board one of them," she said, never taking her eyes off the people who crossed back and forth across the concourse.

"Like the subway, you mean?" Jack asked.

"Something like that," she smiled.

I looked to my left and could see the concourse had a ticket booth in the centre of it with a four-faced clock. It didn't have any hands so it was impossible to know what time it was. That seemed a little fucked up to me, as how would anyone know what time their train was leaving? It was then that I noticed there weren't any windows or doors, so it was impossible to know whether it was night or day outside the station. I looked up and could see departure boards with their bright luminous lights which dazzled my eyes at first. It took me a while to see the destinations listed. I scanned the gleaming rows of orange writing and saw that one of the trains departing from platform 41 was destined for a place named Sydney. Sydney? I thought. Sydney, Australia?

I looked at those in line. Nobody seemed to notice anyone else. Although the station was a hive of activity, no one stopped to talk, chat, or pass the time of day. I got up from the bench and headed towards the ticket office. It was made of wood, just like the one I had seen in the station where Isidor had died. I reached the end of the line, and standing back, I peered through the glass window. The ticket seller was a wizened-looking black man, who sat at the counter behind a sheet of grubby-looking glass. Although his hair was white and curly, and his faced lined with age-defying wrinkles, his eyes were keen and sharp – like there was a younger person staring out from behind his ancient face.

'"What is your destination?" he asked, taking a glass bottle of Coke from the counter he sat behind and raising it to his craggy lips. The red and white label fixed to the bottle looked as faded and wrinkled as the man who drank from it.

'"I'd like to go to Sydney, please," I heard someone say. I looked at the front of the line and could see a guy in a police uniform speaking through the glass at the ticket seller. He had crumbs down the front of his uniform and what looked like a crumpled packet of Jammie Dodgers poking out of his police coat pocket.

The ticket seller cocked his head to one side and said, "Sorry officer, did you say you wanted to go to Sydney?"

"That's right," the cop said, looking through the dirty panel of glass at him. "How much is that, because I don't have any money."

'"There is no charge," the old man said, pushing a ticket through a gap between the glass and the counter.

'"Thank you," the cop whispered, looking down at the ticket. It was blank on both sides. Looking back through the glass, he said, "There is nothing written..."

'"Have a safe and pleasant journey," the old man winked back at him. "Next!" he then hollered to the person standing behind the young cop.

I watched the cop walk slowly away from the ticket booth, turning the ticket over and over in his hands as he made his way down the escalators and beneath ground towards platform 41. I lost sight of him amongst the crowds, or did he just simply disappear? I headed back to the bench. Sitting back down next to Lilly, and with my flesh feeling chilled, I said, "Are all these people ghosts?"

Chapter Eight

Potter

"They're all dead, if that's what you mean," she said, glancing at me, then back at the crowds. "Some of them just sit as if waiting for someone to join them on their impending journey. Others are rushing for their train as if late for some important meeting. They can't wait to board one of those trains below ground. When I first discovered this place, I don't know how long I sat here watching the dead hustle and bustle about, queue at the ticket office and take drinks from the vending machines. Like any new place you visit, like your first day at a new school or in a new job, you soon figure out how things work. I knew I was dead."

"Dead?" Jack said, giving her a sideways glance.

"I knew from the moment I opened my eyes and discovered I wasn't lying in a shallow grave in the forest where my killers had hidden my body," she explained. "I heard the sounds of those guards' whistles coming from deep below ground and I knew that I was dead. Just like you, I could hear trains and was dazzled by the bright departure boards. Eventually I plucked up the courage to leave this bench and slowly approach those departure boards. I thought I might make a journey, like so many of the other dead people seemed to be doing. I noticed that one of the trains departing from platform 63 was heading for a place named Ozstralia. I thought some of those little twinkling lights which made up the letters of the words on the departure board must be broken and the name of the train's destination should have been called Australia. I'd never been to Australia and had always wanted to visit. And suddenly, like the new kid at school, I thought I had everything figured out. I was getting a second chance to do all those things, go to all those places I hadn't visited when alive. So I joined the queue for the ticket office and waited in line. I didn't have any money and was dressed only in my fur coat, which I had died in. Nobody seemed to notice this. Nobody seemed to notice anyone else.

"'What is your destination?" the ticket clerk with the ancient-looking face and bright eyes had asked.

"'I'd like to go to Australia," I said, looking through the dirty panel of glass at him.

"Did you say *Oz*-tralia?" the old black guy asked, raising one wrinkled and gnarled hand to his ear.

"Yes," I mumbled, feeling confused myself at that point. "But I don't have any money."

"'There is no charge," the old man said with the sweetest smile I had ever seen.

"'Thank you so much," I said, taking the ticket he'd slid beneath the glass. With a frown, I noticed the ticket was blank on both sides. I looked back through the dirty glass at the ancient ticket seller and said, "There must be a mistake – this ticket is blank."

"'Have a safe and pleasant journey," the old man winked at me.

As I sat and listened to Lilly tell her story, I knew I had just seen the very same thing happen to the cop who had wanted to travel to a place called Sydney.

"I was hustled away from the ticket office by the next dead person in line," Lilly continued. "I made my way beneath ground. Other than me, platform 63 was deserted. It seemed like I was the only person who wanted to go to *Oz*-tralia that day. I didn't have to wait long until a grand-looking steam train chugged into the platform, plumes of thick smoke pouring from its funnel. The train came to a halt, its pistons and brakes hissing and spitting. The carriages looked old, Victorian, and made of wood.

"'All aboard!'" someone hollered from deep with the engine smoke, which had now shrouded the platform like fog.

"Reaching up, I opened a carriage door and climbed on board. Despite the ancient look of the carriages, the seats where soft and comfortable. I took my seat as the train started to slowly chug forward. I was asleep even before the train had cleared the platform," Lilly explained.

"Where did you wake up?" I asked.

"Not in *Oz*-tralia or Australia, that's for sure," Lilly said, looking at me.

"Where then?" Jack asked, staring at her, eyes wide.

"I was deep below ground. In a place with a person I had long since forgotten," she said. Then looking at me, she added, "I was in place called The Hollows and watching *The Wizard of Oz* with my friend Jim Murphy."

"Murphy," I whispered, remembering how my friend had once told me that he had taken Lilly – Pen – deep into The Hollows to watch one of the many magical-moving pictures the Vampyrus named Burton had brought from above ground.

Before I'd had a chance to say anything, Lilly continued. "But it wasn't like I was really there. It was like I was watching through a crack in the wall of The Hollows. And when me and Murphy went above ground and into the secret forest, it was like I was watching myself with Murphy through gaps in the branches of the trees. It was then I realised that I wasn't really there somehow – I was like a ghost able to revisit my past life, to take another peek at it through cracks. But then I would wake up here again, in that comfy Victorian train carriage, down on platform 63 where I had started my journey. But I wanted to go back. I wanted to see and remember more. So I got in line and waited just like I had before.

Reaching the ticket booth, the old guy with the wrinkled face said, "'Let me guess, you're going to *Oz*-tralia again?"

"'Sure am,' I smiled at him through the dirty glass panel.

"He punched me out another blank ticket and I headed straight back to platform 63 again. The steam train drew into the station and I boarded it. Time and time again, I went back to what I now called *Oz*-tralia until I got to that time in my life where I was murdered by my lover Marc and his brother," Lilly explained.

"But Murphy told me that they hadn't really killed you," I said frowning. "He said that you were only unconscious..."

"That's what I told Murphy," Lilly cut in. "I *was* murdered and I woke up here in this station like I've already explained. But every time I went back, those cracks got bigger until eventually I could touch and speak with Murphy again. I wanted to be with him again, but how could I even begin to explain that I was dead – that I'd come from nowhere – through a crack? Our time together was going to be short. We made a bed by placing my fur coat on the forest floor and then we made love. It was after this I made up my lie. I told him that Marc and his brother only believed that they had murdered me when in fact I was really alive. In my heart I didn't know when I would next return from the station and if I would be able to reach out to Murphy again. I'd heard rumours that most people could only reach through the cracks once, others more, but for most it was only the one time. So sensing this was the one and only time I would ever have to touch or speak with him again, I told Murphy I had to go on the run and that's when I created the name Lilly Blu. If I were ever able to reach for him through a crack again, I would leave him a message in a newspaper signed in my new name. But on my return to the station, I realised I was carrying Murphy's children inside of me. Unable to return to Murphy myself, our children were taken back through the cracks where they belonged and left with their father. I didn't run out on him or my daughters like Murphy has believed all this time. I loved Murphy and my daughters and still do. But why had I remembered him? Why had that word *Oz* appeared on the departure boards? It was like someone or something had pricked a hole in my death and my past life was shining through somehow," Lilly said.

As she said this, I thought back to the conversation I'd had with Murphy on discovering him to be back in this *pushed* world. He had described this world as being like a sheet of tracing paper which had been laid over the world we had been *pushed* from. He said the love letters which I had sent to Sophie in my old life had shown up in this world because a hole had been made in the tracing paper and they had bled through.

Staring straight at Lilly, I said, "Murphy told me that the old world – before it got *pushed* – is starting to make holes in this world and it shouldn't be. He said it was like a really bad thing to happen."

"Murphy's here?" Lilly said, leaping up from her seat. "He got *pushed* into this world, too?"

"Well, yeah," I sighed, not knowing if I'd said the right thing or not. Probably not – knowing how often I opened my mouth and fucked things up.

"Did he get the message I left for him in the newspaper yet?" Lilly asked, wringing her slender hands together in her lap.

"What message?" I said, looking up at her. "What newspaper?"

"The piece of newspaper Sam has," she said. "It's on the back of that article Sam has about Kayla being murdered by her father, Doctor Hunt, in the mountains."

I remembered Murphy showing me Kayla's headstone in that graveyard and telling me how Hunt had murdered both her and Isidor in this world. He had believed them to be winged creatures from below ground. Murphy had suspected that Hunt had somehow remembered this from the world before it had been *pushed*. I now wondered if Murphy had been right in what he'd told me. Perhaps Hunt had started to remember? Perhaps cracks had started to appear in his life. Just like Lilly – Pen – had revisited Murphy by stepping through the cracks.

"Has Murphy seen the newspaper clipping?" Lilly asked again.

"I don't know anything about any newspaper clipping, and as far as I'm aware, neither does Murphy," I sighed, desperately trying to fit together everything I'd learnt from Murphy and was now learning from Lilly. I knew all the pieces must fit together – but how?

"Is that news clipping important?" Jack said, looking at me, then at Lilly.

"Probably," Lilly breathed, slowly sitting down next to me again. She looked deeply shocked. Scared.

"Are you okay?" I asked, still not sure if I should have said anything about Murphy or not.

"Murphy was wrong," she whispered, looking at me, her eyes wide and bright.

"About what?" I asked.

"The holes he was talking about, although I call them cracks, they are a good thing," she said.

"How do you know that?" I said, feeling confused. "Who told you?"

"The same person who carried my daughters in that cardboard box back to Murphy," she said.

Both Jack and I stared at her blankly.

Lilly looked over her shoulder in both directions, as if fearing that some enemy might be eavesdropping. Then, leaning in close to me and Jack, she whispered, "The old guy in the ticket booth told me. He said if we want to *push* the world back, we have to make as many cracks as possible. We have to destroy this world."

Chapter Nine

Jack

"How would a simple ticket seller know so much?" I asked, loosening the bandana about my neck. In fact, how did the old black guy with the wizened face and fuzz of white hair know anything? I'd been back in this world two hundred years or more and what Lilly was explaining was all new to me.

Lilly shot a glance over her shoulder back towards the ticket booth where the old guy continued to punch out tickets for the never ending stream of dead travellers who waited in line. The marble floor seemed to tremble beneath my feet as the sound of arriving and departing trains rumbled deep below ground. Lilly leant in close again, like a coach giving a halftime briefing, and said, "His name is Noah, and he's not just a ticket seller — he is way more important than that. He knows pretty much all there is to know about the worlds being *pushed* — but not only that, he knows about this station and the others scattered about this world."

Both me and Potter shot a glance at the ticket booth and the old guy sitting happily behind the glass.

"So he's like the Yoda of the railways?" Potter said, looking back at Lilly and popping a cigarette into the corner of his mouth.

"Yoda?" Lilly said with a curious stare. "I said Noah."

Potter shook his head, and jetting streams of blue smoke from his nostrils, he said, "Forget it, sweetheart."

Why did he always have to be such a fucking jerk? I wondered. I glared at him, then turned my attention back to Lilly. "So how does he know so much?" I asked her.

Lilly looked back over both shoulders in turn again, then back at us. Just above a whisper, she said, "Noah is an Elder."

"That would account for all the wrinkles," Potter cracked, cigarette dangling from the corner of his mouth.

Growing ever more frustrated at Potter's infantile attempts at humour, I hissed, "If you can't keep your fucking mouth shut, why don't you do both me and Lilly a favour and fuck off..."

"Okay... okay," Lilly breathed. "Let's try and keep this nice, shall we?"

"Well, he's starting to piss me off," I scowled. "Why does he have to keep coming out with dumb fucking remarks the whole time...?"

"Who are you calling dumb?" Potter shot back at me. "I was just saying that what Lilly said made sense, as I've seen under those Elders' hoods and their faces are so freaking wrinkled and old, they've had to be stitched back together."

"You're such a lying bas..." I started, but Lilly cut over me.

"And why do you think they look like that?" Lilly asked the both of us.

Potter shrugged and I remained silent. I didn't know the reason.

"They are literally falling apart – they are dying," Lilly started to explain.

"So what about the old dude in the glass box?" Potter said, grinding out his cigarette on the marble floor with the heel of his boot. "He looks ancient, but he isn't quite falling apart – not yet, anyway."

"Noah isn't like the other Elders," Lilly said. "He has always been different from the others, that's why they eventually banished him. The four remaining Elders are cruel and full of pain. In fact, that's how they feed – that's how they survive and have done so since time began – by living off others' fear, unhappiness, and pain."

"But I always thought they had the different species – the humans, the Vampyrus' – best interests at their very hearts," I said.

"That's what they've wanted you all to believe," Lilly said.

"Their hearts are black and twisted like shrivelled prunes," Potter said. "I saw those too under their robes when they brought me back."

Potter spoke with a sudden seriousness as if something had clicked into place for him.

"You're right, Potter," Lilly said, looking at him. "There is no love in their hearts. Every decision they have taken since the beginning of time hasn't been for the benefit of the humans or anyone else. The only people they have helped are themselves. Life was only created so they could feed off its misery and pain. They enjoyed the fact that the humans and the Vampyrus fought over the Earth."

"So why separate the two species from each other? If what you are telling us is true, then wouldn't they have got a kick out of us destroying ourselves?"

"And once both races were dead, what then?" Lilly said. "No, the Elders had to keep both races alive, but in misery and in pain. The Elders learnt that some mixing had taken place between the Vampyrus and humans, so they forbade it. They fed off the misery caused by separating those that had fallen in love. But in time, even those humans and Vampyrus who had once loved forgot each other and their hurt and pain grew weaker. So what then? How would the Elders survive if the two races forgot about one another? They needed to be reminded again. So a little boy named Elias Munn was chosen. Unbeknown to him, the Elders made sure the boy discovered a hole between the two worlds. And as the Elders hoped, Elias Munn fell deeply in love with a human. And when Elias was rejected by her, he tore out his lover's heart and the Elders gorged themselves on his heartbreak and torment. They stood back in the shadows and watched Munn cause mayhem for hundreds of years as he slowly encouraged other Vampyrus above ground, where they infiltrated human cites and fed off those living there. Again, members of the two different species fell in love and had children – the half breeds. Again the Elders forbade those relations and fed off the pain that caused."

"But what about us, Lilly?" I said, rubbing at my narrow temples with my fingers. "They afflicted us with the Lycanthrope curse because we murdered women and children. Isn't that exactly what the Elders would've wanted?"

"And has our race stopped killing now that we're wolves?" Lilly asked, staring straight back at me.

"No, we kill more," I said thoughtfully.

"Exactly," Lilly sighed deeply. "Not only do the Elders feed off the pain and suffering of our victims, but now they also suck on the pain and torment we feel as we struggle with the curse. They sold us a false promise that if we stopped killing then the curse would be lifted, but they knew we would never beat it. Look at the pain and suffering the curse has caused us. As wolves, we've struggled our whole lives to kick the habit of killing. The Elders are now getting twice as much pain and suffering than before they cursed us – when we were just killers. We were enjoying murdering – but not any longer. Our pain has become as great as our victims'. The fun has been taken out of it. The Elders can't afford for anyone or anything to have too much fun for too long."

"And I thought you two were a couple of evil motherfuckers," Potter said, looking at us. "You look like a couple of freaking saints compared to the Elders."

"I'll take that as a backhanded compliment," I barked at him.

"Take it anyhow you like," Potter said, lighting another cigarette.

"But what I want to know is where Kiera fits into all of this? Why does she have to choose between the humans and the Vampyrus?"

Lilly looked at Potter and said, "Where there is darkness, there must also be light," she said. "You can't have one without the other. Noah knew that and that's why he was banished. He was the light shining brightly on the Elders' dark plans. Noah knew that it was inevitable that at some point in time, someone would come who wouldn't give in to the Elders' hate and pain. This person would be strong, show courage, and always look to the light when thrown into darkness. The Elders knew that such a person would be dangerous if he or she managed to set a shining example and get others to follow. They suspected that if ever such a person should come, then they would have to have more strength than just a mere human or Vampyrus, and would therefore be the best of both species – a half breed or half and half. This only made the Elders more intent on forbidding mixing between the humans, Vampyrus, and Lycanthrope," Lilly explained.

"But despite their manipulations and cunning, Kiera came," Potter said thoughtfully, cigarette smoke lingering around his fingers.

"When they discovered how resilient Kiera was when they saw how she would never hate and could overcome any obstacle, then they knew she was the one they feared," Lilly said. "But in their twisted hearts, they realised that perhaps her kindness and love could be their strength."

"How?" I asked her.

"At first they were happy to linger in the shadows and watch Luke Bishop – Elias Munn – try and break her, but his plans were thwarted because she fell in love with you, Potter, and not him."

"You can't blame her, I guess," Potter said with that cocky smirk of his.

Like me, Lilly ignored his comment and continued. "The Elders knew they had to get Kiera to choose between the two races – the humans and the Vampyrus," she said.

"But why?" I asked.

"Because she's a half breed," Lilly said, and both me and Potter shared a brief knowing glance. "For Kiera to make a choice between the two different sides would be like a mother choosing between her two children. Now if Kiera had made that choice, can you even begin to imagine the pain, the guilt, the torment she would have felt forever more knowing that she had destroyed an entire race of people – her people – whichever way she made her choice? The Elders would've fed off her pain for an eternity."

"But I thought it was Luke who was making her choose," Potter said.

"The Elders wanted him and you to believe that," Lilly explained. "They were manipulating Luke because they knew he was evil, greedy, and weak. They could never let anyone know it was their wish and plan alone for Kiera to choose. Why do you think Kiera had to make her choice in the Dust Palace? The Elders wanted to be there when she did so. They wanted to see the pain in her eyes – get a whiff of her anguish and trap those feelings of despair in their lair."

"But Kiera wouldn't be manipulated by Luke, and she didn't choose. She sacrificed herself by throwing herself at me," I said, remembering how she had run towards me in the Dust Palace. "She would've rather have died than cause anyone else pain."

"And the Elders were furious," Lilly whispered. "They wanted to punish her for what they saw as her trickery. But they also needed her."

"Why?" Potter asked before I'd the chance to ask the very same question, which was on my lips.

"From what I've heard, this Kiera Hudson is like no other – she is unique," Lilly said.

"She is," Potter cut in again, his jet-black eyes clouding over as if picturing her in his mind.

I thought of her, too, and how she had had such an effect on me in the little time I had spent with her in that room. Even though I had tortured and killed her father in front of her, even though I was threatening to kill the man she loved and her friends, she still wouldn't give up on me. It was like she saw something in me that I couldn't *see*. Anyone else in that very same position would've killed me – had their revenge for everything I had done to them – but not Kiera. Even though I could see she was in pain at the sight of her father dying before her, she hadn't given in to that pain and killed me, handed me over to Potter and Murphy who were coming for me. It was like even in the darkest hour of her life, she had seen some flicker of light. Had she seen that flicker of light in me? I wondered.

"The Elders realised that those that love the most hurt the most," Lilly continued. "So they weren't quite finished with your friend Kiera Hudson yet. The Elders bought her back..."

"So they could fuck with her head," Potter said, sounding angry.

"Not my choice of words, Potter, but yes, you're right," Lilly said. "As Jack tore Kiera to pieces in the Dust Place before the Elders, it was like her life – her very soul was unravelled for them to see. It was then they saw everything – what Kiera truly was and how they had been deceived. And for the first time it was they, the Elders, who felt pain and misery as they learnt how they had been deceived by Murphy."

"So the Elders know that Kiera is like us?" I asked Lilly.

"She's nothing like you two," Potter snapped.

Ignoring him, Lilly said, "Yes, they know where Kiera came from and who and what she really is. The Elders didn't like the fact they had been tricked – conned, they felt despair and they started to fall apart beneath their robes – it was like they were being unravelled. So they decided to punish Kiera. They wanted to cause her so much pain they hoped it would help to heal them. So they *pushed* her into this world where she would learn about her father, her mother, her brother, and what she really was. They would make sure she discovered what a liar and a cheat the man she loved was," Lilly said, casting an eye at Potter sitting next to her on the bench.

Potter looked down at the ground and Lilly continued.

"They wanted Kiera to learn that Murphy had kept secrets from her, they wanted her to see her father die all over again." And this time Lilly looked at me. "They sent Kayla and Isidor back because the Elders knew how much they were like a brother and a sister and they wanted Kiera to see them die all over again. They wanted to *push* Kiera into a world of pain so they could feed off her, like rats gnawing at a corpse."

"So that was just a bunch of bullshit about us being angels sent back to help Kiera?" Potter asked, crushing out another cigarette and lighting another almost at once.

"Yes," Lilly said with a nod of her head. "They needed you all to believe in this new world. They wanted you to think you had a purpose other than to cause Kiera pain – because it wasn't just about Kiera's anguish – it was about all of your pain, too."

"So my name isn't really Gabriel?" Potter asked, his eyes wide and hopeful. "Because I can tell you, being called that has been pretty fucking painful. Murphy hasn't stopped taking the piss."

"Being sent back has been more than just about a name," Lilly said, sounding exasperated with Potter. I knew how she felt. "They wanted you to not only feel pain yourself – but also cause pain for Kiera."

"I'd never hurt Kiera," Potter growled as if he were being accused.

"How's Sophie Harrison?" Lilly shot back.

"I didn't go looking for her to hurt Kiera..." Potter spluttered, coughing up a lungful of smoke.

"Going in search of your past lover hurt Kiera though, didn't it?" Lilly said. "Not only did it hurt Kiera, it caused you and Sophie pain. How much hurt was Sophie caused by remembering you and then knowing that she couldn't have you?"

"That's pretty goddamn spiteful," I said, enjoying seeing Potter squirm.

"You hurt her, too," Lilly said, snapping her head around to look at me. "You went to her house in your search for Kiera. You murdered Marty, her boyfriend in this world."

Now it was my turn to drop my head.

"You twisted sonofabitch..." Potter started.

"That's before any of this," I howled, raising my head to look at the both of them. "I did that when I hated Kiera – when I wanted her dead for deceiving me in The Hollows. That's before I spent time with Kiera at her father's house..."

"Where you made her watch you kill him..." Potter cut in.

"Enough already!" Lilly barked, raising her hands like a referee separating two caged fighters. "You've both screwed up – we all have. But sitting here and pointing the finger of blame isn't going to stop the Elders. And it certainly isn't going to help Kiera. Now grow up – the pair of you."

We sat in silence. I breathed deeply as I tried to control my rage. I was pretty much angry the whole time, but Potter really knew how to push my buttons. I sat and watched the dead rush for their trains or join the line for the ticket booth. Just as I felt the seething rage ease within me, Potter opened his mouth again.

"So if you're right and the Elders are feeding off all of our pain, especially Kiera's, don't you think someone should go and tell her I'm not really dead? I mean, I'm not bigging myself up, but she looked pretty fucking distraught when she thought she saw me die back in Wasp Water."

"No," Lilly said. "For now Kiera has to believe you're dead, as do your friends. You're right, the Elders will be enjoying this – they will be almost high on her despair – so high that they will take their eye off us and what we're really planning."

"And what is that?" I asked her.

"To unmask the photographer," Lilly said right back with a knowing smile.

Chapter Ten

Potter

I had seen the photographer once before. Whoever was hiding beneath that hoodie had snapped a picture of me holding the dead body of that wolf boy – Dorsey, I think his name was. Whatever, I'd been set up by the dickhead sitting on the bench next to me and Lilly. That photograph had been used to convict me and send me to the guillotine.

"Ask your friend who the photographer is," I said to Lilly, pointing at Jack. I really didn't know if I could trust either of these wolves. I'd put my trust in the Lycanthrope before and got myself in the shit. Why should it be any different now?

"What's that s'posed to mean?" Jack snarled back at me.

"Oh come on, Jack," I glared back. "You set me up with that wolf teacher and her sidekick pupil. You got the photographer to share a Kodak moment with me and the dead boy."

"I set you up because I wanted Kiera to see what a lying-cheating little turd you really are," Jack said. "I didn't ask the photographer to photograph you with the dead boy. I was kinda hoping that those two wolves were going to tear your freaking heart out."

"I got a good fucking kick-in, thanks to your mate," I said to Lilly, remembering how those Skin-walker cops had turned up and beaten the shit out of me in the snow.

"Look, we can sit here forever more blaming each other for events that have happened in the past," Lilly said, looking frustrated with the both of us. "But it's not going to solve anything. If we are going to *push* back, you two have got to learn to accept that for now, you're on the same side – on the same team."

Jack looked at me and I looked away. I didn't know if being on the same team was possible for me and Jack. But I bit my tongue and said nothing more. I would suffer his company for now, only because it would help Kiera. There was no other reason, and deep in my heart I was never gonna trust him and I was gonna keep my wits about me around Lilly Blu. After all, both of them were wolves. Then, trying to ease my aching conscience a little, I looked at Lilly and said, "You know it wasn't just me going in search of Sophie that made her remember the world before it got pushed. Somebody had been sending her those letters I had once written to her. Was that the photographer, too?"

"Yes," Lilly said.

"But why send those letters to Sophie?" I asked. "What was the point?"

"What was the point in you going to find her again?" Lilly came back quickly at me.

"Because..." I started.

"Because you still had feelings for her," Lilly cut over me. "Noah believes that the photographer wanted to awaken the feelings that Sophie once had for you, so when you came together again you would resume that love affair. Now can you imagine how much pain that would have caused..."

"Kiera," I whispered, before she had a chance to finish. "But I stayed true to Kiera."

"When that didn't work, a picture with the word *push* was left in Kiera's flat for you or her to find, it didn't matter who, as long as it worked its way back to her," Lilly said. "The photographer knew the picture would awaken Kiera's feelings for her father and she would go in search of him. With the word 'push' written on the back, Kiera would somehow believe it was her destiny to find her father again. Get a second shot at some happiness. After all, she had found little to be happy about in this new world."

"But that photograph led her to me," Jack grunted, his crazy yellow eyes fading in brightness. It was something close to a look of remorse – something I had never seen in the evil bastard's eyes before.

"What do you mean?" I asked him.

"That picture the photographer left for Kiera or you to find in her apartment wasn't of her father, it was of me looking like her father," Jack tried to explain. "I took on Frank Hudson's form to bait Kiera into the house so I could take her hostage and tell her that she was my sister. She was so pleased to see me – or who she believed to be her father – that she threw her arms about me. It was then the photographer appeared in the front doorway and took the photo of us together."

"Weren't you just a teeny-weeny bit suspicious?" I sneered, unable to let go of those feelings of mistrust I had for Jack deep inside of me.

"No, not really," Jack said, his eyes still dull-looking. "I'd heard Luke mention the photographer before and I thought it was all just part of the trap we were setting for Kiera at that time."

"So whoever this photographer is, he's working for Luke and the Elders?" I said.

"Not necessarily so," Lilly said. "Noah thought the same at first and so did I, but now we're not so sure."

"He must be," I insisted. "Whoever it is, he or she is going around sending letters and taking pictures to remind us of our past lives. It was one of those photographs that led Isidor to his death. This photographer left a picture of Isidor and the girl he loved in a grate leading down into The Hollows. So don't sit there and try and tell me that this photographer is nothing more than a piece of scum."

"Perhaps Isidor's death was an accident," Lilly said.

"Look, lady, I'm not known for my sense of humour, so stop trying to be funny," I growled at her. "That picture led to Isidor dying, and that's another thing I have to feel guilty about."

"More pain," Lilly said thoughtfully. "Guilt isn't an easy thing to live with."

"Stop the psychotherapy session, I'm not in the fucking mood," I said. "I made my peace with Isidor before he died. So don't sit there in judgment – you're not so freaking perfect yourself."

"So why has the guy in the ticket booth had a change of heart about the photographer?" Jack suddenly said, as if it was now his turn to diffuse the growing tension, not between us, but between Lilly and me.

Lilly looked at him and said, "At first it was believed that the photographer – whoever it is – was assisting the Elders by provoking old memories in you all, so you sought out your past lives and relived the pain there."

"Whoever it is has done a great job," I said, unable to hide my bitterness.

"But Noah noticed that perhaps delivering the letters and taking photographs has had a positive effect on this world," Lilly said.

"Watching my friend Isidor have his head ripped off by a bunch of filthy wolves isn't what I would call positive," I said.

"No, but the holes – the cracks – that the letters and pictures made are a good thing," Lilly said.

Both Jack and I looked back at her blankly.

"Those letters made a hole or a crack in this world, in which the old world could shine through," Lilly said. "So in a way, Murphy was right. He saw it too, and like Noah and me, at first he thought those holes being made in the tracing paper were a bad thing, but they're not – they're very, very good."

"Why?" Jack asked, leaning forward on the bench and staring at her.

"Because those holes and cracks are weakening this world that the Elders pushed you into," she said, dropping her voice to a whisper again. "The more of us who remember our past lives, the more holes appear in the tracing paper. What if there were eventually so many holes that more and more of us could see through to what the world used to be and should be like? What if the humans started to remember? Do you think they would sit back and let their children be taken to those schools for matching? Do you think Luke and the wolves would be running the show for much longer if they remembered what the world used to be like?"

I looked away from Lilly and out across the station. I watched the line of dead people wait for their ticket to travel. I looked at

Noah as he happily punched each of them out a ticket. Then slowly turning my head to look at Lilly, I said, "This is what this station is for. This is what Noah is doing. Every time he gives out one of those tickets and these people make journeys back into their past lives, they are pushing open holes in that tracing paper that separates the two worlds."

"Exactly," Lilly nodded with a smile. "Noah is making cracks. With each journey that is made, more appear until this whole *pushed* world the Elders created falls apart, revealing the one underneath. And just like I remembered Murphy and my past life, so will everyone else remember theirs, too."

"So if Noah and you have all this figured out, what are me and Jack doing here?" I asked.

"Whoever the photographer is, he or she is passing through the cracks. They could be waiting in line right now. So we need you to unmask this photographer so we can discover if he or she is working for us or against us," Lilly explained.

"If you don't know where to find the photographer, how do you expect me and Potter to know where he is?" Jack asked, and he was rubbing his temples again with his fingertips as if suffering a migraine.

"You might not know where the photographer is now," Lilly smiled, "but you know where he has been."

"So... what? I'm gonna somehow go back to the day he took a picture of me with the dead wolf boy and unmask him?" I scoffed. "Is Jack meant to rip back the photographer's hood as he's taking a picture of himself and Kiera?"

"You've got the plan kind of half right," Lilly said. "Neither you and Jack can go back and come in contact with yourselves. Noah says that would be really, really bad."

"So if we can't go to where and when we can be sure the photographer will appear, how the fuck are we meant to catch him?" I quizzed.

"You said that the photographer left a picture for your friend Isidor in a grate leading down into The Hollows," Lilly reminded me. "You also said that he left a picture of Kiera and her father in her apartment. So there are two times and places you know for sure the photographer will show up."

"So you want us to go back together?" Jack asked, his eyes now shining brightly again.

"Not together," Lilly said. "We don't have time for that – and besides, what if you both missed him? We only have one shot at this. We stand a better chance of you finding the photographer if you split up."

I was still trying to get my head around what it was Lilly was asking me and Jack to do, when she stirred me out of my thoughts by touching me on the shoulder and saying, "Potter, you go back and wait for the photographer to place the picture in Kiera's apartment." Then turning to look at Jack, she added, "And you, Jack, go back to the place where the photograph was placed for Isidor to find. One of you is sure to discover the identity of this photographer."

"But I haven't got a clue where this grate is going to be..." Jack started to protest.

"I know where it is – well, I can point you in the right direction at least," I said, trying to remember the story Isidor told us. "You need to find a place called Lake Lure. Isidor and his girlfriend, Melody Rose, used to sit and read by the lake there."

"Sounds like a right barrel of laughs," Jack snarled.

"Find Isidor and you'll find the place where he used to creep out from The Hollows and where the photographer leaves the picture for him," I said, getting to grips with the plan.

"And what about you?" Lilly asked me, a look of concern on her face.

"I think I can find Kiera's apartment all right," I said. "It will feel strange to see her again. I wonder how different she will be..."

"This isn't some kind of jolly," Lilly snapped. "You're not to have any contact with Kiera. She isn't the Kiera you know and love. That's not why you're going back through the cracks."

"Murphy told me that Kiera got shot dead attending a robbery," I said.

"So?!" Lilly said. "Don't concern yourself with that. Don't get involved with the Kiera Hudson of the *pushed* world. Don't interact with her or change anything. Unmask the photographer and come back." She stared at me then added, "If you don't think you can handle not getting involved with Kiera, then I'll send Jack in your place and you can go and find the grate..."

"I can handle it," I said, standing up. "I don't think we should send Jack, do you? What, with his record for rape and murder."

"She's my sister," Jack barked, jumping up onto his long spidery legs.

"Didn't stop you in the Dust Palace," I shot back. Before he could come back at me, I eyed Lilly and said, "So let's get this over with. How do we go back through the cracks?"

Looking at me, Lilly said, "Get in line like everyone else and get yourself a ticket."

Chapter Eleven

Jack

If that prick made one more jibe about me being a killer, I was going to tear him a new arsehole. He had done his own fair share of killing in the past. Potter was far from perfect – but he strutted around the goddamn place as if his shit didn't stink. He had left as much shit in his wake as I had. I was glad we were splitting up. The mission would have lasted five freaking minutes if it had been me and him traveling back together. Only one of us would have come back through the cracks Lilly had spoken about, and it wouldn't have been that obnoxious prick.

I got in line behind Potter. Lilly stood beside me. Being seven foot tall, I towered over those ahead of me. I could see the line snaking away. I glanced at those who wandered about the huge concourse. So many dead people. A thought struck me which made my heart race: Would any of my victims be here? Were any of those women I had previously slain be waiting to get a ticket to go back? Would they recognise me? Sure they would – I was the last thing they saw as I ripped them to pieces. Would they want to speak to me? I doubted it. But I would love to speak with any one of them. It would be fascinating to talk with them about what I had done to them. I rubbed my temples with the tips of my bony fingers again. I could ask them what It had felt lIke to be scared by me. What had that fear felt like for them? Was there a little part of them which had secretly enjoyed what I'd done?

"*Stop it, Jack,*" I whispered to myself, pushing those thoughts away.

But maybe some of my victims did find their death as much as a rush as I found killing them, I wondered. Maybe there was something in that fine line between pleasure and pain.

"*Stop it,*" I whispered again to myself and swallowed hard. I didn't want to think like that anymore. If only those thoughts would go away. Leave me in peace.

"What did you say?" Potter said, jerking his head around to look at me.

"Nothing," I scowled at him.

He turned away again with a shrug of his broad shoulders.

"Are you all right?" Lilly asked, placing one hand gently on my forearm. "Are you struggling?"

I knew Lilly would understand my conflicting feelings – she was a wolf after all. I wondered how many she had killed in her life – or had she managed to beat the curse? Killing is like crack – you do it the once and spend the rest of your life chasing that original high. Now wasn't the time to ask. I had to get my demons in check if this mission was going to be a success. I couldn't risk everything by going on a killing spree on the other side of the cracks and holes Noah and the photographer had been making. But those thoughts – cravings – just wouldn't go away; they never truly did. Killing to me was as natural as breathing air. The cravings were always there, sometimes weak, other times, strong. It was like they rippled over me in waves. As I stood in line, those waves of desire to kill had grown suddenly strong, and like always, I didn't know how long it would be until they faded again. The quickest way for them to go was to make a kill – but I didn't want to do that anymore.

"Are you sure you're okay to do this?" Lilly asked, her hand soft against my arm.

I looked down into her sparkling eyes. She smiled at me, her lips red and full, snow white hair jostling about the curve of her smooth neck and shoulders. I looked away. I didn't want her to see in my eyes what I was seeing in my head. I didn't want her to see how much I wanted to take her – hurt her. Wolf or not, killing her would be so fucking sweet.

"*Stop it*," I told myself again, opening and closing my hands. They felt hot and clammy as I drove away the images of tearing open her white fur coat and enjoying myself on what lay beneath.

"You did say something?" Potter said, swivelling around to look at me again. "I know this is like a really dumb question, but are you okay?"

"I'm fine," I growled down at him. "I just want to be left alone."

"That's fine with me," Potter said, looking front again.

With Potter's back turned to us, Lilly touched my arm again and said, "Jack, I don't think this is such a good idea. I don't think you should go back."

I brushed her hand away, I couldn't bear her touch. It made my heart race way too fast and created those pictures in my head. Although I enjoyed seeing those images of me and Lilly together, I couldn't risk looking at them for too long, or the mission would be over for me and Lilly.

"Don't touch me," I whispered.

"I want to help you," she whispered back.

"No, you don't want to help me," I said. The only help she could give me right now would be to let me take her then kill her. "I don't need your help, Lilly Blu. I'll be fine to go back through the cracks."

"If you're sure," she said, looking at me.

Without looking down and meeting her stare, I said, "Is there a chance that any of my victims could be here, trying to get back?"

"I don't know," she said. "Why do you ask?"

"These are dead people, right?" I said.

"Sure," Lilly nodded.

"So is my brother, Nik here someplace?" I said, not wanting to talk about those women I had once killed.

"I don't know," she said. "He could be anywhere."

"Is anywhere like *nowhere*?" I asked, and this time I did risk looking at her.

"There are smaller stations that people travel through," Lilly said, her eyes growing wide as they met with mine.

I looked quickly away as I saw myself yank open her fur coat in my mind. "So I might never see my brother again?" I asked. "He might be dead to me forever."

"Yes," Lilly said softly.

"He was all I had left," I said. "Nik was good for me. We helped each other. He is the only family I had left."

"You have Kiera," she said.

"She won't want to know me, if and when this is all over," I told her. "Kiera is too good for me. She's better than me."

"Do you know for certain that's how Kiera feels?" Lilly asked me. "You need to ask her."

"I need to keep away from her," I said, still unable to bring myself to look at Lilly. I just wanted those images and thoughts that plagued me to stop. "I will just end up destroying her."

"You need to tell Kiera this..." Lilly started.

Then, reaching into the back pocket of my jeans, I pulled out a crumpled envelope and thrust it into Lilly's hands. "If I don't come back... if I fuck up or something goes wrong... give this letter to Kiera for me."

Not giving Lilly a chance to say anything, I looked back at the line as Potter reached the ticket booth.

Chapter Twelve

Potter

I peered through the glass partition at the wrinkled old black guy. His eyes twinkled like stars beneath a set of overgrown white eyebrows. His face was a map of deep, ragged lines. They spread out from the corners of his eyes, down the sides of his ancient face, and formed what looked like a spider's web around his mouth.

"And what is your destination, Potter?" he asked with a brilliant smile.

"Where do you suggest?" I shot back at him through the glass.

Noah brought a dusty-looking Coke bottle up to his dry-looking lips and took a sip. The red and white label around the centre of the glass bottle was faded and peeling away. "Have you not checked the departure board for destinations, Potter?"

I glanced to my right and scanned the hundreds of boards with their twinkling orange lights. One board seemed to be lit up more than the others, as if drawing my attention to it. I checked out the destination. *Very cute,* I thought to myself with a half-smile. Looking back through the glass at Noah, I said, "I've heard the Hudson River can be very nice at this time of year."

"Did you say *Hudson*?" the old guy asked, bringing an arthritic-looking hand up to his ear.

"Yeah, that's the place," I said.

Noah punched me out a ticket and pushed it beneath the glass partition. "Have a safe journey, Potter, and I hope your stay at the Hudson River is a productive one."

"I'm sure it will be," I said, taking the ticket and turning it over in my hands. And just like I guessed it would be, the ticket was blank. "Thanks..." I started, looking back at the booth.

"Next!" the old guy shouted over me.

I stepped to one side so Jack could approach the ticket booth. Jack arched his skinny back, stooping so he could look through the glass at Noah.

"What is your destination?" Noah asked Jack, just like he'd asked me.

"You tell me," Jack barked.

Easy, tiger, I thought to myself.

Still smiling, the old guy peered at Jack from inside the booth and said, "Can't you see any place you would like to go to?"

Stooped at the waist, Jack turned his head and glanced over at the departure boards, then looked over at me. "What did you say Isidor's girl was called?"

"Melody Rose," I told him.

Looking back through the glass at the old guy, Jack said, "I'll take the train that's departing from platform 12."

"And where is that train heading?" Noah asked, screwing up his eyes and peering up at the boards.

"The Rose Garden," Jack said.

"Sounds very picturesque," Noah said, punching out a ticket and sliding it towards Jack. "Lots of beautiful pink roses."

Jack picked it up with his long, tweezer-like fingers and inspected it. "Who said the roses were gonna be pink?" Jack grunted.

"I'll wager they are," Noah smiled brightly back at him.

Without saying anything, Jack turned away from the booth. And instead of Noah shouting the word 'Next' like he had so many times before, he called after Jack and said, "Be careful of the roses, Jack, they can have thorns. Make sure you handle them with care."

"I'll be careful not to cut myself, if that's what you're worried about," Jack said over his shoulder.

"It's not you I'm worried about, Jack," Noah said, his smile fading. "Make sure you don't hurt one single petal on any beautiful roses you might find."

Jack fixed the old guy with a knowing stare, then looked away again. Turning the ticket over in his fingers, he joined me and Lilly.

"What's that crazy old fucker going on about?" Jack said.

Looking him straight in the eye, I said, "You know exactly what the old guy means, and don't forget it, Jack."

Jack broke my stare, and I couldn't help but feel a sense of dread. Was sending a fucking serial killer back to watch over a fourteen-year-old boy and girl the sanest thing in the world to do? I wanted to warn Jack not to hurt either of them, just like Noah had, but before I'd the chance to say anything, he was striding away on his long, spindly legs towards the platform where the train for The Rose Garden was departing from.

Lilly looked at Jack stride away and said to me, "Are you ready to go, Potter?"

"I guess," I said.

Then turning to face me, she said, "Don't change anything. Just find this photographer and come back." Lilly leant forward and kissed me gently on the cheek.

I watched her trot off across the concourse after Jack.

"How do I get back?" I called after her, waving the ticket in my hand.

"Find a station," she said, glancing back with a smile. Then she was gone, heading down the escalators after Jack and onto platform 12.

"What freaking station?" I muttered, looking down at the ticket I held between my fingers. Sliding it into my coat pocket, I made my way across the concourse and towards platform 56. I stepped onto the escalators and travelled below ground. About halfway down, I looked back and the concourse was nothing more than a pinprick of light above me. I looked front and could see what appeared to be a well of darkness opening up beneath me like a set of jaws. But it wasn't total darkness down there. There was a murky kind of orange light. Reaching the bottom, I stepped off the escalator and onto platform 56, which was lit by a series of gas lamps. There was a draft as the flames in the lamps flickered back and forth. There was no one else on the platform other than me. I looked left and right and there was a tunnel at either end of the platform and both were thick with darkness. Water dripped from the ceiling and the walls were stained green with damp. A rat scurried out of the darkness and clambered over my boot. I kicked it away and onto the tracks.

Then, out of the corner of my eye, I saw a flicker of movement at the far end of the platform just before the opening of one of the tunnels.

"Hello?" I called out.

Whoever it was made no reply.

"Do you want to see my ticket?" I shouted, fishing it from my coat pocket. The sound of my voice echoed off the surrounding walls. As my voice faded away, I heard the sound of wind blowing through the tunnel. It was strong and cool, blowing my hair back from my brow. As the rush of the wind grew stronger and louder, so did another sound. The platform began to tremor and the tracks made a hissing sound as a steam train headed out of the darkness of the tunnel. It was black and it raced forward, looking like a giant beetle in the darkness. Clouds of thick, grey smoke poured from its funnel. The windows of the cab were black so I couldn't see in and get a glimpse of the driver. Jets of steam spat from beneath the wheels as the driver – if there was one – put on the brakes and the train shuddered to a stop in the platform. The enclosed platform soon filled with the smoke that still poured from the funnel of the engine. I glanced to my right and saw that figure again, like a shadow amongst the smoke.

"All aboard," I heard a voice come from deep within the smog. The voice was childlike, and I was sure I heard whoever it was snigger excitedly.

"Who's there?" I said, squinting into the thick smoke. "Don't you wanna see my ticket?"

"All aboard," the childish voice said again, and this time whoever it was did giggle, the sound was unmistakeable and chilling.

With gooseflesh breaking out like a rash all over me, I reached out and tugged at one of the carriage door handles. I climbed inside, pulling the door closed behind me with a thud. Just like Lilly had described, the inside of the carriage looked like something you would see in a museum. The seats were covered in a thick purple cloth with a gold trim. The frame of the carriage was made of a dark coloured wood. I fell into my seat as the train suddenly lurched forward, then left and right. The driver blew on the horn, and the sound was deafening. This was followed by the sound of a whistle being blown on the platform.

Leaning forward in my seat, I pulled down the window set into the carriage door and peered out. Again, I could see the murky shadow of that figure shrouded deep in the smoke billowing from the train. From within the clouds of smoke slid a small white hand. The tiny hand waved at me, as that childlike voice whispered from the smog, "Goodbye, Potter."

I sat back in my seat, my heart suddenly racing and the sound of giggling fading away behind me on the platform. Even before the train had reached the confines of the tunnel, I felt my eyelids become heavy. I tried to stop them falling shut over my eyes, but it was impossible. I closed them for just a second and snapped them open again. The carriage was now in total darkness and the motion of it swaying from side to side had stopped. The train must have come to a sudden halt in the tunnel. But there was something else. It took me a moment to realise what. There was someone in the carriage with me.

"Who's there?" I asked, half expecting to see that paper white hand slide out of the darkness.

"I could ask you the same thing," someone said back.

A light came on and I snapped my eyes closed at its sudden brightness.

"Potter!" the voice gasped. "Where do you get off breaking into my apartment after what you did to me?"

I opened my eyes to find myself looking up into Kiera's hazel eyes. Before I'd had the chance to say anything, she had rolled her fist back and punched me straight in the face, just like she had so many times before.

Chapter Thirteen

Jack

I stepped onto the escalator, then felt someone tug my arm. I looked back to find that Lilly had caught up with me. I eased my arm free of her grip. Those cravings to kill had eased a little. But still, I didn't want her to reignite them. I looked at her, knowing that she wouldn't see anything other than my crazy yellow stare.

"Are you sure you want to do this?" she asked me.

"Yes," I nodded. "I have to."

"Are you doing this for Kiera?" Lilly said.

"No, I don't think so, not really," I said thoughtfully.

"For who then?"

"Me," I told her.

"Why?"

"It's not often someone as evil as me gets to go back and put something right," I said, turning and heading down the escalator. It made a chugging noise beneath me as each step cranked around on a rusty chain.

"Jack!" I heard Lilly call to me one last time.

I glanced back over my shoulder at her.

"Be good," she smiled, then turned her back on me and disappeared amongst the crowds on the concourse. Turning to look down into the approaching darkness, I knew I couldn't promise to be good, but I would certainly try. If I didn't make it back, I was content to know that Lilly had the letter I had written for Kiera.

I stepped onto the platform. It was dark, and I could only make out the edge of the platform because of a strip of fluorescent lighting overhead. It made a fizzing sound as it flickered off and on like flashes of lightning. Moths fluttered about the blinking light. The walls of the platform were constructed from a rusty coloured brick. There had once been posters attached to the walls, but all that was left were strips of faded paper. There was a wooden sign hanging from the wall. All but one of the screws fixing it had come loose. So the sign which read 'The Great Wasteland Railroad' hung lopsided from one corner. Shouldn't that have read 'The Great Western Railway'? I wondered. I couldn't be sure. I couldn't be sure of anything anymore. All I knew was I couldn't afford to fuck this journey up. I had to get through it without killing anyone or thing. Lilly had made it clear that I wasn't to interact with anyone or change anything other than unmask the photographer. Maybe if I could do this without killing, then I would start my own journey towards beating the curse that caused so much pain, not only to my victims, but me, too.

I caught sight of someone further up the platform. I couldn't see them clearly, it was too dark. The strip of lighting above me flickered on and off, and the person, whoever it had been, was gone again. A humming sound filled the tunnel to my right, sounding like a swarm of angry wasps heading my way. A single light appeared deep within the tunnel and got bigger with every passing moment. The humming sound grew louder as the light got bigger. A train raced out of the tunnel. It wasn't a steamer like Lilly had described. The train was electric, although I couldn't see any overhead cables or third rail running alongside the tracks. The engine was made of metal and was pointed like a snow cone at the front. Its once-white body was now covered in sheets of flaky rust. The cab windows were so cracked, they appeared frosted. It was impossible to see who the driver might be. I stepped towards the carriages and could see that each of them, like the engine, looked weather-beaten and old. There was a whooshing sound as the carriage doors slid apart.

"All aboard," someone said.

I looked to my right to see a woman crawling up the platform. Peering into the gloom, I realised that she wasn't crawling at all, but clawing her way along the platform on her belly. She had no legs, and a stream of black blood and entrails dragged behind her where she had been ripped in half. She looked like she was wearing a tattered and torn wedding dress.

"Climb on board," she gargled on a throat full of blood, which spurted over her lips and onto the platform. Her hair looked black, or was it simply coated in blood? I couldn't be sure.

"Do I know you?" I asked her.

"You killed me, Jack, on my hen night," the woman gurgled.

It was then I remembered the young woman and her friends. I remembered how I had slaughtered each and every one of them. I got no pleasure at watching her crawl up the platform towards me, her eyes white and rolled back into her skull.

The sound of the doors closing snapped me out of my trance. I looked up and slipped between the narrow opening and into the carriage. The doors closed behind me. I pressed my nose against the window. The woman was now standing on the platform. She wore a perfectly white wedding dress, a veil pulled down over her face. In her hand she held a small posy of pink roses.

She raised the hand holding the posy and waved at me. "Be good, Jack," she whispered as the train started to ease its way out of the station.

I lost sight of her as the train started to gather speed. It rocked from side to side as if going over a set of badly maintained points, and I fell backwards onto the seat. It was surprisingly comfortable and my bony arse sank down into it. At once I started to feel tired. I couldn't remember ever feeling so sleepy before. I struggled to keep my eyes open as the train slid into the tunnel. My eyes closed and my head rocked forward as I fought the tiredness. I snapped my head back and opened my eyes. I was still in the tunnel but no longer on the train. It was like the carriage had disappeared all around me. I wasn't sitting either, but crouching. The tunnel I was now in wasn't wide enough for a train to pass through, let alone allow me to stand up. The tunnel walls were covered in mud – no, they were made of mud, as was the ground I was kneeling on.

"Where the fuck am I?" I breathed.

There was a noise ahead of me. I crawled forward on my hands and knees into the darkness and followed the sound. It sounded like someone was crawling through the tunnel ahead of me. I rounded a bend and stopped. There was a boy on his hands and knees. He was heading upwards towards a spot of light. It was then I realised where I was and who I was following. I was back in The Hollows and crawling after Isidor as he made his way above ground.

Chapter Fourteen

Potter

"What was that for?" I cried, jumping out of Kiera's armchair and standing up. I put my hands to my face for the second time that day to stem the flow of blood gushing from my nose.

"That was for running out on me, Potter!" Kiera seethed behind me.

"Running out on you...?" I muttered, the warm sensation of blood flowing through my fingers stirring me awake somehow. Where was I? More importantly, *when* was I? I glanced around the apartment and realised I had been here before. This is where I'd come after leaving Hallowed Manor... after I'd gone in search of Sophie... this is where I'd discovered that picture of Kiera and her father. I glanced over at the table where I'd taken it from. There wasn't any picture and I guessed the photographer hadn't left it here yet.

"Don't act all innocent," Kiera said, now standing in front of me, hands on her hips. She was wearing her white police work shirt and black police issue trousers. "When you put in for that transfer to 'C' Division – you knew what you were doing... you were running away, Potter!"

"Running away..." I mumbled through the blood that was now congealing on my upper lip and chin. What the fuck was she talking about? And then like another sudden punch to the face, I realised I wasn't talking to the Kiera I knew and loved, but the Kiera from this *pushed* world – the Kiera Lilly Blu warned me not to have any contact with. Had I fucked up so quickly? Sure I had – that was my style. I fucked everything up one way or another. It was what I was good at – my claim to fame. I had made fucking up an art form.

"How dare you stand there and pretend you don't know what I'm talking about!" she said, stepping forward and pushing me in the chest with the balls of her hands.

I staggered backwards. She was truly pissed at me. Two different *whens* and *wheres* and nothing had changed very much. I still had the knack of making Kiera Hudson mad at me.

"Really, I don't know..." I started, then stopped. How did she know my name and who I was? This was the first time we had met. I hadn't come into contact with Kiera in this *pushed* world... not unless... unless... unless? I staggered backwards again, but not because I had been pushed by Kiera, but because of what was slowly dawning on me. I dropped back into her armchair by the tall bay window. Was there another Potter... another *me* in this *pushed* world? Had Kiera fallen in love with this *other* Potter? Christ, two Potters running around in the same world causing mayhem – things really were fucked up!

"Get up and get out!" Kiera snapped at me, hooking her thumb towards the door.

"Hang on, just hang on a minute," I breathed, arming away the blood from beneath my nose. "I'm not sure I understand what's going on here."

"I think it's perfectly clear to see what's going on here, Potter," she seethed, showing no signs of chilling out. "When you walked out on me over a year ago, you said you needed some space... some time on your own to get your head around things... you promised you would be in touch. But I didn't hear a word from you... not so much as a postcard. All I did was say 'I love you' and you ran for the hills..."

"You love me?" I said, still trying to play catch-up and figure out what kind of relationship the Kiera and Potter from this world had shared.

"The word you're searching for is *loved!*" she snapped. "I did love you, but not anymore, Potter. I have so gotten over you."

"Really? I ran for the hills because you said you loved me..." I breathed, feeling really rather shocked. The Potter from this world seemed to be a bigger dickhead than me. I didn't know if I should be pleased about that or not.

"Don't you dare sit there and pretend there's another reason you pulled the vanishing trick," Kiera said, pointing her forefinger at me like a cop telling me my rights.

"I'm sure I didn't run out on you because you said you loved me…" I started.

"So there was another reason, was there?" she snapped, her long, black hair falling about the sides of her pale face. "What was it, another woman?"

Was there another woman? How the fuck should I know. I wasn't responsible for this other Potter. "No, there wasn't another woman," I said, looking straight back at her. "There could never be another woman like you, Kiera."

"Oh, my God," Kiera breathed out loud. "I don't believe what I'm hearing."

"Believe what?" I said, noticing the thousands and thousands of newspaper cuttings tacked to her apartment walls. This Kiera wasn't so different to the Kiera I knew.

"You think you can waltz back into my life, pay me a few cheap compliments, and I'd fall straight back into your arms," she said, her eyes wide with disbelief.

"I'm not here to pay you cheap compliments…" I started.

"So why are you here, Potter?" she demanded, tapping her foot restlessly on the carpet.

That was a good question… but how did I answer it? I couldn't tell her the truth. "Erm… Erm…" I said, struggling to find an answer.

"You're so full of shit, Potter," Kiera said angrily. She reached down, took hold of the sleeve of my long black coat, and yanked me from her armchair.

"Look, I'm sorry…" I mumbled, my brain still racing to find the right words.

"It's too late for sorry," Kiera said, shoving me towards the front door of her apartment. She yanked it open. Staring out into the hall and not at me, she added, "Don't ever break in to my home again, Potter, or I'll have you arrested, even if I have to do it myself."

I stepped out into the hall, and even before I'd had the chance to turn around and look back at her, Kiera had slammed the door shut behind me.

"Well, that couldn't have gone any better," I said under my breath, heading down the hall and out of the apartment block.

I stepped out onto the street. It was night and there was a fine drizzle in the air. Pulling the collar of my coat up around my neck, I headed into the darkness. I knew I couldn't go too far from Kiera's apartment block if I were to try and catch the photographer. I would have to stay close by and keep watch on the apartment. But where could I hide? There were plenty of trees in the street, but if Lilly Blu thought I was going to hang out in a tree, she was sorely mistaken. I knew I was something close to a bat – but that was just taking the fucking piss. Then, in the light of an overhead streetlamp, I saw a narrow alleyway set between two houses across the street from Kiera's apartment. I headed across the road into the alleyway. With the drizzle becoming a steady downpour, I leant against the rain-soaked wall and watched Kiera's apartment block. I hoped the photographer put in an appearance sooner rather than later.

I took one of the cigarette packets I had stolen from the machine at the campsite from my coat pocket. I poked a smoke between my lips and tried to light it. Within seconds, the cigarette was little more than a soggy white stick as it soaked up the falling rain. I tossed it to the ground. This mission was turning to shit with every passing minute.

From my hiding place, I peered up at Kiera's window. I saw the lamp light she had switched on go out. Was she going to bed? I wondered. Then, the front door opened, and Kiera appeared in the doorway. She was now wearing blue jeans, white T-shirt, and a waist-length black jacket. Kiera pulled the front door closed behind her and ran through the rain to a little red Mini parked at the kerb. I watched Kiera climb inside, turn on the headlamps, then start the engine. The car pulled away from the kerb and disappeared into the night.

Where was she going? I wondered. I reminded myself that whatever the Kiera in this *pushed* world did had nothing to do with me. She wasn't *my* Kiera. But still, I was more than curious to know where she was going and what she was going to do when she got there. I stepped from my hiding place and glanced up the street. I could see the red taillights of her small car disappearing in the distance. Looking back at the apartment block, I knew I should stay and keep watch and wait for the photographer to show up. I looked again up the street and could see no sign of Kiera's car. I looked back at the apartment block.

"Bollocks," I whispered, rolling back my shoulders and releasing my wings.

Throwing my head back and spreading wide my jet-black and tatty wings, I shot up into the night sky after Kiera. I scanned the streets below, until I saw her car weaving its way through the narrow streets of Havensfield. She was heading towards town. I swooped overhead, hidden by the rain-filled clouds. With rain beating off my wings, I followed Kiera's car until she pulled into the kerb and parked. Folding back my wings, I dropped sharply out of the night sky, landing behind some rubbish bins at the rear of a drab-looking pub. I could hear the sound of muffled laughter and conversation coming from inside.

With my wings withdrawing back into me, I headed around the side of the pub and onto the street. I peered around the side of the building to see Kiera climb from her car. She had parked outside a small Italian restaurant. It was then I saw someone step out from the shadows and approach her. All my instincts urged me to race across the road and protect her. I stopped myself. I saw Kiera turn around and smile sweetly at the man who had approached her. She then stood on tiptoes and kissed the guy gently on the cheek. The guy offered her his arm, which she took hold of as he led her smiling into the restaurant. It wasn't the fact I'd seen Kiera kiss another man and take his arm that troubled me – well it did if I were to be honest – but it was the man himself. I stepped back into the shadows, my heart racing.

"John Miles?" I whispered. "Kiera Hudson is dating that fucking werewolf, *Sparky!*"

Chapter Fifteen

Jack

I followed Isidor at a safe distance as he crawled ahead of me. He reached the patch of pale white light, and I heard a wailing sound like unoiled hinges squeaking. I screwed my eyes into slits and could see Isidor was lifting back some kind of grill in the ground. Isidor hoisted himself up through the hole and disappeared above ground. On my hands and knees in the filthy mud of the tunnel, I crawled up towards the grill. Just before reaching it, I heard it swing back into place, as Isidor closed his entrance to the world above ground. I heard the sound of his feet head away. I waited for the thud of his footsteps to fade, then made my way towards the grill. Sliding my fingers through the bars, I pushed it up and open. I poked my head through the hole and peered out. There was what looked like a small woods, and in the distance I could see Isidor weaving his way through the trees, his back to me. It was winter above ground and bitter cold. Isidor was stripped to the waist. Didn't he own a freaking coat? I wondered. The kid must have been freezing cold. Potter had always said the kid was dumb – perhaps he had been right about that one thing. I heaved myself out of the hole, and standing, I closed the grate. Looking at it, I guessed this was the place Potter had spoken about. This was where the photographer was going to leave the picture for Isidor to find. I stepped back away from the grate, and from behind a nearby tree, I stood and looked at it. How long would I have to wait for the photographer to show up? I wondered. Was it going to be hours? Days or weeks? How the fuck should I know? Then I remembered Potter saying that the picture was of Isidor and his girlfriend Melody Rose who had died. The picture surely then wouldn't be placed in the grate until after the girl's death or what would be the point? Was this girl dead already? Again, I didn't know. Looking in the direction Isidor had headed, I knew there was only one way to be certain, and that was to follow the boy to discover exactly what the fuck was going on. So just like I had in the tunnel down in The Hollows, I followed Isidor at a distance as he made his way through the woods.

Isidor reached the treeline and I hung back. I watched him step out onto a sandy shore, which circled a lake. In a strange way it reminded me of the Dead Waters, hidden deep within the secret forest. I guessed this was Lake Lure Potter had mentioned. So far, so good, I figured. From my hiding place near the edge of the woods, I watched Isidor sit in the sand as the cold, black-looking water lapped at his feet. He shivered with the cold, wrapping his arms about his shoulders. It was then I noticed that the boy didn't have the tattoos I had seen on him before. They must have come later. He didn't look like the kind of kid that would go and have angry-looking black flames engraved all over his chest and up his arms and neck. He definitely didn't look like the sort of kid who would have eyebrow piercings. Isidor looked like the sort who wouldn't say shit even if his mouth was full of it. Something must have happened to change him, I figured. I don't know how long I hid in those woods, but the winter sun started to drop on the horizon as if it were sinking beneath the lake and down into The Hollows. Then, from behind me, I heard a rustle and the sound of snapping twigs underfoot. I spun around, wondering who it might be. There was a young girl making her way through the woods towards the lake. I slunk back behind the trees and watched her. She had dull, light coloured hair, which she had dragged back into a bun. The girl wore what looked like a grey coloured bonnet on her head and this was fastened beneath her chin with a black cord of some kind. She looked sickly pale and she wore a long, plain dress, which matched the colour of her bonnet. Over the dress hung what appeared to be an apron, and on her feet she wore the most uncomfortable-looking shoes I had ever seen. She clomped forward in them through the trees and I watched her go. So this was Melody Rose? Fuck me, what did Isidor see in her? The kid was fucking dumb. He killed himself for that? I wondered in disbelief. And everyone said I was fucked in the head. I'd kill the girl – but jeez – to get my kicks, she had to be at least semi-attractive.

The girl reached the shore, and I saw Isidor look around at her. At first his young face beamed with delight at seeing her. Shit, he really did have the horn for her in a bad way. He needed to come on a night out with me. I could introduce Isidor to women who would do things to him that would make his hair and toes curl. But then his face seemed to change as it took on a more sullen look. At last he's finally realised what a hag she is, I thought with a smile.

Melody said something, which I didn't quite catch. Pricking up my ears, I dared to inch closer through the trees to the shore.

"I waited all morning! I was freezing, Melody!" I heard Isidor bitch.

Being cold was the least of his worries, I thought.

"I'm really sorry," Melody said, touching his arm.

"So you gonna tell me what you've been up to?" I heard Isidor ask.

Possessive too, I grinned. He really did have the hots for her. I would've killed the bitch if she had stood me up. Where was this kid's fucking backbone?

"Aw, c'mon, I've said I'm sorry, haven't I?" Melody smiled at him.

Don't smile sweetheart, I grimaced. *It really doesn't do you any favours. It makes your face look like a plate with a crack in it.*

"It's not the fact that I was left waiting in the cold. I ran into Ray and his friends and they stole my coat," Isidor groaned.

So that's why the kid wasn't wearing a coat, I realised. But that didn't explain why he wasn't wearing it now. He must have let whoever this Ray dude was get away. What was wrong with this kid? You don't let anyone steal from you. If anyone tries, you rip off their fucking face then go around and have some *fun* with their entire family while you force the thief to watch. Jeez, this boy needed to toughen up. What a pussy! He needs to spend some quality time with Uncle Jack, I smiled to myself.

"Poor Isidor. No wonder you're so cold." I heard the girl sigh.

Oh, my God, I thought. These two fucking deserve each other. "Poor Isidor," I mimicked under my breath. "Tell the fuck-wit to toughen up – to be a man, for Christ's sake. What is wrong with these kids?"

Then, as if I were unable to believe what I was seeing, the girl stepped forward and gently wrapped her arms around Isidor as if trying to warm him. They gazed into each other's eyes. Clutching at my stomach, I crouched down behind the tree I was hidden behind and vomited. Ropy lumps of puke and bile swung from my chin and I cuffed it away with my hands.

"Jealous, Jack?" I heard someone say over my shoulder.

I glanced back and fell straight onto my arse at the sight of the bride standing amongst the trees a few feet away. She held the posy of pink roses in her white-laced glove-covered hands.

"Don't you wish you had someone to hold and love like that?" she said just above a whisper. The veil that hid her face moved like it was caught in a gentle breeze as she spoke from behind it.

"Fuck you," I breathed through clenched teeth. I wiped the hot puke from my chin and stood up. I looked back at where the bride had been, but she had now gone. She had never been there, I told myself. Coming through the cracks had messed things up. It had fucked my head up. That was the last thing I needed. I knew I had to find this photographer and get back before I completely lost my mind. I looked back through the trees to find that Isidor and Melody were no longer standing on the shore. I came out from my hiding place, and being careful just in case both Isidor and Melody were still close by, I stepped out on to the sandy shore. It was then I saw both of them crawling through a nearby clump of bushes, set back against the treeline.

"Good boy," I whispered with a smile. Perhaps I had underestimated Isidor and he was taking the girl into the bushes for some humpty-dumpty. This I had to see, I thought, crouching low and heading towards the bushes Isidor and Melody had disappeared into. Noah had told me not to hurt the girl. But had he seen her? He described the rose as being beautiful. He must have been talking about someone else entirely. This girl was no freaking rose, she was more like some annoying weed. Reaching the bushes, I crouched low. I was surprised to hear Melody giggling.

"Are you laughing at me?" I heard Isidor ask. He sounded hurt.

Don't say he has a small pecker too, I thought. You couldn't make this shit up. Didn't the boy have anything going for him? No brains and no cock!

"Well, it's kind of a dumb thing to do, don't you think?" Melody giggled again, unable to figure out what she meant. Then she added, "Who would choose a book if they didn't know what it was called or what it..."

Book? I wondered. Who takes a book on a freaking date? Perhaps it's porn? But I doubted it somehow.

"You think I'm stupid, just like the others do," I heard Isidor say.

Yep! I thought to myself.

"Oh, my God, Isidor, I didn't realise. You didn't know what the book was about because you couldn't read the title, could you?" the girl said from the other side of the bushes.

"No," Isidor said back.

Oh this just keeps getting better and better. I didn't know whether to laugh or cry for the boy. Not only had he been robbed of his coat, not only did he have a small dick, but he couldn't read, either. No wonder he had brought a porno book to read, they could both just sit and look at the pictures.

"I don't think you're stupid," I heard Melody say to Isidor.

You must be about the only one who thinks that, I thought.

"I think you are the sweetest guy that I've ever met," she continued, and my stomach lurched again. "You are the only person in this town who doesn't avoid me because of the way my mother makes me dress. Even the people in church keep away from us. No one dresses the way we do. You didn't judge me, Isidor, and I'm not judging you. You helped me mend my necklace, you went and chose a book for me – it had a rose on it just like my name. No one has ever done anything like that for me."

The book definitely wasn't porn. I'd never seen a porno book with a rose on the front. The idiot had probably bought her a

90

gardening manual. Shit, he couldn't read, was he freaking blind, too? I wondered. When I thought I couldn't stomach any more, the conversation took another turn for the worse.

"Why did you laugh then?" Isidor asked her.

"Because I wanted to cry, but I just couldn't let it show," she whispered.

"Why did you want to cry?" Isidor asked softly.

"Because I just can't stop hurting... that is..." she stopped mid-sentence.

"What?" he asked her. "What stops you hurting, Melody?"

"You do, Isidor," she said. "When I'm with you, I stop thinking."

"Thinking about what?" Isidor whispered.

"Come with me and I'll show you," Melody said, and I heard them heading out of the bushes.

I slunk back into the growing darkness and watched Isidor and Melody head away, hand in hand, up the shore.

"What would stop you from hurting, Jack?" I heard someone whisper.

I looked back over my shoulder to see the bride slowly walking away from me and back into the woods, where she disappeared again.

"Fuck you," I breathed, shutting my eyes.

Chapter Sixteen

Potter

"Sparky!" I whispered in disbelief again. He was a freaking werewolf. What was Kiera dating him for? Not only was the guy covered in zits and wore those crooked-looking glasses, he couldn't be trusted. He had led Luke and the others to Hallowed Manor where they had killed and slaughtered the half-breeds – two of which had been Murphy's daughters.

Part of me wanted to sneak across the road and peer in through the restaurant window, just to make sure I had seen what I thought I had seen. But what was the point? My eyes hadn't lied to me. Kiera – for some unknown reason – had hooked up with Sparky. Had the Potter in this *pushed* world treated Kiera so badly she had lost all faith in men and fallen into the arms of Sparky? I'd also been away from the apartment block for far too long already. What would be the point in coming back to endure seeing Kiera with another man – *Sparky* – only to miss the photographer and go back empty-handed? Heading back behind the pub, I rolled back my shoulders, released my wings, and tore up into the night sky. The night air was cold against my face, and the rain jabbed it like ice-cold pellets. I soared over the town of Havensfield and headed back to Kiera's apartment. However much I tried, I couldn't get that picture of Kiera kissing Sparky out of my head.

He was a fucking wolf!

But was he a wolf in this world? I suddenly asked myself. People were different here, weren't they?

Once a wolf, always a wolf! I told myself.

But I knew I couldn't be sure of that. Was the Potter in this world a Vampyrus? No – they didn't exist here. Wolves did, though. The place was overrun with them. Should I warn Kiera somehow? No I couldn't. Lilly told me not to get involved with the Kiera Hudson of this *pushed* world. She wasn't my Kiera. No, she was Sparky's. I'd already screwed up by waking up in her apartment. But was that my fault? Had I had any control where the train *pushed* me through the cracks? I didn't think so. Whatever, I should keep out of this Kiera's life. What she chose to do was her problem – not mine. I should concentrate on getting back to my Kiera and making things right for her. This Kiera had nothing to do with me. The Potter of this world had had his shot, and by the sounds of things, he had fucked up. That was his problem – not *mine*.

Convincing myself not to get involved, I landed back in the alleyway opposite Kiera's apartment. The lights were still out. Was that a good sign? Had I missed the photographer? I doubted he would have walked into Kiera's apartment and switched on all the lights, lighting up the place like a freaking Christmas tree. All I could hope was that I hadn't missed him – *her*? The rain had eased a little, so I took my pack of cigarettes from my coat pocket and lit one. The warm rush of smoke felt good as it filled my lungs. I tried not to think about Kiera and Sparky, but whenever I closed my eyes, all I could see was Kiera reaching up on tiptoe and planting a soft kiss on Sparky's zit-ridden face. It wasn't that I was jealous – how could I be? I didn't love that Kiera. I was just concerned about her and I didn't trust Sparky in this *pushed* world or any other, for that matter.

"Why are you so concerned about someone you don't love?" a voice said from behind me. It was childlike and I knew I had heard it someplace before. I spun around to discover a little girl standing at the other end of the alley. She waved at me with a hand that was as white as a fish's belly. I knew at once that it was the little girl who had been hiding in the smoke on the platform.

I pitched out my cigarette and slowly headed up the alley towards her. "Hey, little girl, what did you say to me?" I tried to make my voice sound as nonthreatening as possible so as not to scare her away.

"You love her, don't you?" the little girl giggled. "Kiera is very pretty."

"She's not my Kiera," I said, continuing down the alley towards her. Now that I had drawn nearer to the little girl, I could see she couldn't

be any older than about seven years old. She had long dark hair that had been weaved into plaits which hung down on either side of her pretty face. Her eyes were as dark as her hair. She wore a red dress, white knee-length socks, and black patent shoes.

"Who are you?" I breathed, coming within touching distance of her.

Raising her corpse-white hand again, she waved at me and giggled, "Be seeing you later, alligator." Then she was gone, like smoke drifting up into the night air.

"Who told you to say that?" I called after the puff of smoke. "Why did you say that to me?"

The only reply I heard was the faint sound of giggling melting away into the distance. Taking another cigarette from my pocket, I sparked it up, then turned back to the entrance of the alleyway. I slouched in the darkness and looked at Kiera's apartment. Her car was back, parked outside the front. She was back already? I thought, flicking away the cigarette I had lit only moments before. Why had she come back so quickly? I wondered. Had she brought Sparky back with her? They couldn't have even had time to order dinner and eat it. Had they come back so soon as they were desperate to jump each other's bones? I feared. I pushed that thought and the images it created out of my head. I lit another cigarette.

I looked up at the windows, but no lights came on. They had gone straight to bed. I dropped the cigarette and ground it out with the heel of my boot. I immediately lit another. She was entitled to sleep with Sparky if that's what she wanted, I told myself, wrestling with the thought of the werewolf running his filthy hands all over her body. I suddenly had the urge to vomit and I tossed another half-smoked cigarette away. I leant against the rain-soaked wall of the alleyway. Even though it wasn't my Kiera in the apartment on the other side of the street, I couldn't bear the thought of her and Sparky having sex. It wasn't right – it wasn't *natural*.

I paced up and down the alleyway, wringing my hands together.

Is this how Kiera felt when she learnt I had sneaked away to see Sophie? I guessed it was, and I felt ashamed. The little girl, whoever she was, had been right, whether the Kiera living on the other side of the street was my Kiera or not – my feelings for her were just as strong – just as raw, and I couldn't bear to think of her having feelings for another man – Sparky or not.

Unable to rid myself of the need to know if Kiera and Sparky were together in the apartment, I stepped from the entrance of the alleyway and crossed the street. I climbed over the front wall and crept around the back of the building. Feeling safe in the knowledge that I couldn't be seen, I released my wings and floated silently upwards. Reaching Kiera's bedroom window, I peered around the edge of it like some kind of peeping tom. And what I saw made my heart ache. Kiera lay on her side, tucked beneath the blankets that covered her bed. She was alone. Her face was turned towards the window, her eyes shut tight against the tears which spilled silently from them. Her body trembled with uncontrollable sobs.

Had she rowed with Sparky? Is that why their date had ended so suddenly? Had he hurt Kiera in some way?

I wanted to force open the window, take her in my arms, and tell her everything was going to be okay, but I couldn't. Not because Lilly had told me to not get involved, but because I couldn't lie to her. I knew everything wasn't going to be okay for the Kiera in this world. I knew that sometime soon, she was going to be shot dead attending the scene of a robbery.

Turning away from the window, I went back to my hiding place on the other side of the street and waited for the photographer.

Chapter Seventeen

Jack

Melody led Isidor into the night and I followed at a distance. To be honest, the pair were so fucking loved-up with each other, I could've walked beside them singing the 'Hokey Cokey' and neither of them would've noticed I was even there. I cringed every time they gazed sideways at each other. As the night grew darker, it got colder. The town I followed the two lovebirds through was closed for the day, and the streets were empty and silent.

I crept behind them as the girl led Isidor across town. At the edge of it, they seemed to suddenly disappear ahead of me. Had they realised they were being followed after all, and ducked into some front yard or alley to avoid me? Slowly, I placed one foot in front of the other and continued forward up the road leading out of town. To my right I noticed a narrow track. I stopped and listened. I could hear them ahead, the sound of their footfalls on the rough, uneven ground. Both sides of the narrow lane were sheltered by trees and I darted into them to keep hidden from view. The moon was now up, and on such a desolate strip of road, should either of them suddenly look back, I would be seen. In the distance on a small hill, I could see the outline of a house set against the starry night sky. Staring ahead and not down at the ground, I tripped on a large fallen branch. I put my hands out and gripped a nearby tree trunk to stop myself falling flat on my face. A bird screeched in the branches overhead and soared away. This was followed by an ear-piercing scream of terror. What had happened? Had the girl, Melody, just been murdered or something? It sounded like someone was in fear of their lives.

Bent double at the waist, I made my way through the bushes and trees as quietly as possible. Isidor and the girl were just inches away from the other side of the scrub which lined the track. I could see Isidor was clutching his chest, a look of dumb horror on his face.

"What's wrong? Isidor?" I heard the girl gasp.

"That bird scared me," he breathed.

"I'm meant to be the girl around here," I heard Melody laugh nervously.

Oh for fuck's sake! I thought. The kid shit himself because he heard a bird flutter its wings. The way he was carrying on, I thought some pervert with an axe and a hard-on had jumped out of the bushes. I just hoped he didn't come across a fluffy-eared bunny rabbit next, or Isidor might just shit his pants like he'd overdosed on laxatives. If I ever got the chance, I knew I had to tie Isidor to a chair and put that movie 'The Birds' on repeat. I smiled at the thought of doing that.

Once Isidor had caught his breath, they moved on in the dark and I followed, hidden by the trees. I guessed the house Melody had led us to was where she lived, as she confidently pushed open the front garden gate and headed up the path. A white fence surrounded the front garden, which was neatly kept. The whole scene was something you'd find printed on a postcard. It all looked too fucking perfect for my liking. There was something about the house that didn't sit easy with me. From my hiding place amongst the nearby trees, I watched Melody push open the front door and flip on the light.

"Holy moly!" I heard Isidor whisper as Melody closed the front door behind them.

I waited in the dark, just in case the girl flashed her tits at Isidor and he came screaming out of the house in fear, leaving a trail of steaming shit behind him. After several minutes of waiting for Isidor to suddenly appear, I crept from between the trees. Keeping low, I made my way around the edge of the white picket fence to the rear of the house. Checking over my shoulder to make sure I wasn't being spied on, I hopped over the fence and made my way across the backyard. As I neared the back of the house, a beam of light seemed to come up from out of the ground. Curious, I crouched and made my way towards it. The light was coming from a basement beneath the house. There was a dip in the ground, and a small wall. I climbed over it, and dropped. There was a window that was hidden from view, and I would've never known it was there if it hadn't have been for the light which had been switched on from inside. Hunkering down so low that I was almost lying on my stomach, I peered through the small grime-covered window. With my face pressed almost flat against the glass, I could see Melody and Isidor standing in what looked like a small basement room... no... what looked like some kind of makeshift church.

And I thought the boy had issues. When are these two kids gonna learn that you don't take books to read on a first date and you never, ever go to church! That has got to be the biggest freaking passion killer I've ever heard of. What was the girl planning on doing, for crying out loud? Was she gonna get on her knees and ask God why he saw fit to send her an illiterate, spineless, and dickless wonder of a boyfriend? Christ, I knew each of us had been given a cross to bear – but Isidor just took the piss. I was starting to feel sorry for the girl. She needed to offload her burden – and quick. But then again, maybe Isidor had his own question to ask of God. Like, why had he been saddled with the Hunchback of Notre Dame masquerading as a freaking nun! In a fucked-up kinda way, Isidor and Melody were made for each other.

Peering through the tiny window, I could see half-melted candles scattered about the place. They had been fixed to the damp-ridden walls and stood on tiny china saucers. I could see two small pews in front of what looked like a makeshift altar. Over this had been draped a crimson piece of cloth. There was a statue of Christ and the Madonna. But the thing that drew my attention was the huge cross which had been fixed to the wall behind the altar. It was massive – big enough to crucify a living person on. I could see Isidor and Melody's lips moving as they spoke to one another, but I couldn't hear what they were saying. Perhaps they were praying. Who knew? And did I really give a shit – not really. If the conversation they were having was anything like the one I'd overhead by the lake, then it would be about as interesting as watching paint dry. After a short time, Melody and Isidor left the weird basement, turning the light out.

Bored already tagging along behind these couple of freaks, I decided that perhaps I should head back towards the grate in the woods. After all, I'd been sent back to watch it, not snoop on Isi-bore and Melody *Doze*. What was wrong with those two kids? I wondered, creeping away from the house and shaking my head in disbelief. They had a perfectly good place to make out down by the lake, and now an empty house to themselves, and what did they choose to do? Read and pray! Un-fucking-believable!

Reaching the treeline, I glanced back at the house and could see that a light had come on in one of the upstairs rooms. A bedroom, perhaps? I wondered.

"So what if she had taken Isi-bore up to her bedroom," I grunted. "She's probably showing him her freaking stamp collection. It ain't gonna get any more exciting than that!"

I stepped off the path and back amongst the trees. It was then I saw the bright glare of headlights coming up the narrow track and towards the house. I hid in the shadows as the car slowly crept past. The car stopped outside the house. A grey haired woman climbed from the car. She was a lot older than Melody, but they dressed the same. She wore an identical grey dress and frumpy old black shoes. Melody's mother, I guessed. I watched her head for the front door and go inside. I looked up at the window where I had seen the light and it had now gone out.

The spider has come home early and caught a fly in the web, I smiled to myself. Now this could be worth hanging back for. Dropping low, almost onto all fours, I slinked over the fence and back across the front yard. A wooden trellis covered in ivy was fixed to the front of the house. Releasing my claws, I climbed it. The same upstairs light came on again, and I flinched backwards from the window. Letting my racing heart slow a little, I peered around the edge of the window frame and into the room. I couldn't see Melody or Isi-bore anywhere, the only person I could see was the woman I had seen moments before climb from the car. She removed the bonnet from her head and the off-white apron which hung over the front of her dress. She then crossed the room and went to what looked like some kind of grotto. In the centre of it stood another statue of the Madonna. The woman came away from the grotto holding a set of beads between her fingers. Not more praying, I feared. I was right. The woman dropped to her knees, and closing her eyes, she laced her fingers before her and started to pray before the grotto. I watched her lips open and close as if she were babbling something out loud. The window was shut and I couldn't hear whatever it was she was saying – *chanting*. Just when I was about to give up and climb back down the trellis, the woman stood up and unfastened her dress.

Now this is more like it, I smiled to myself. Or perhaps not!

The woman stood in the centre of the room wearing underwear which was something close to a pair of freaking bloomers! Was I ever going to catch a break? Her skin was covered in more wrinkles than a sackcloth, and her tits sagged so much I feared she might just trip over them as she made her way towards the bedroom door. It was then I noticed her back was covered in a maze of scars.

Now she didn't look like the kinda woman that paid to get spanked, so she must have caused those scars herself. Kinky, I grinned as she left the room. Then, just when I thought things couldn't get any more bizarre, Isi-bore and Melody burst out of the wardrobe and fell back into the room.

"What the fuck is going on?" I breathed, watching as Melody pushed Isi-bore towards the bedroom door. I didn't have to hear whatever it was she was saying, I knew she was scared because of the fear I could see in her eyes. They both left the room, and I quickly climbed back down to the ground. Just as my feet touched the ground, the front door flew open. I pressed myself flat into the ivy covered trellis.

"Who's there? Melody is that you?" I heard her mother screech from inside the house.

Isi-bore appeared on the small porch before the front door. The dull light from the hallway cast long shadows over his young face, making him look older than his years.

"Come with me, Melody. I can take you home with me – it's different – but better than here," I heard him say, his voice sounded desperate and panicked.

"I can't," Melody said.

"Melody! Melody! Who are you talking to? *Who's there?*" her mother screeched again from inside the house.

"It's okay, momma. It's just me," Melody called back, and I could hear fear in her voice. She was scared of her mother.

"Please, Melody, come with me?" Isi-bore pleaded just above a whisper.

"I can't come with you, Isidor," she said, and although I could see her face, I knew that she was crying by the broken sound to her voice. Melody swung the front door closed, leaving Isi-bore alone on the porch.

I watched the boy slowly make his way down the garden path back along the track towards town. He walked with his head bowed forward and shoulders slumped. I followed him. He looked as if he had a very heavy cross to bear.

Part of me wanted to catch up with him and shake some sense into him, tell him not to be such a pussy and to grow up. But there was suddenly another part of me that felt different, watching his lonely figure head across town and back towards the woods. From a distance, I followed him back to the grate. It made a grinding noise in the silence of the night, as he lifted it open. He dropped inside the hole, and closed the grate over his doorway into this world.

"Remind you of anyone?" a voice suddenly asked.

I looked around to discover the bride standing between the trees just a few feet away. Her long, white dress made a whispering sound in the freezing cold breeze.

"Fuck off," I hissed, and took my place behind a nearby tree, so I could watch the grate and wait for the photographer.

Chapter Eighteen

Potter

For two days and nights I froze my nuts off hiding in the alleyway opposite Kiera's apartment. With each passing hour, the cold seemed to work its way through my flesh, until my bones felt like brittle sticks of ice. I was almost out of cigarettes too, as I had pretty much worked my way through the packets I had stolen from the campsite. I had eaten little over the last couple of days, the only food I had managed to find was a rat I had caught scurrying around in the dark. The blood had been hot and sweet, and had gone a little way to help my cravings, but there was no Hollows in this world to go back to should the cravings become too much.

My hunger had only been made worse, when the night before last, I'd seen Sparky arrive on foot carrying a bag of takeout. I could smell the noodles from across the street and my stomach had performed cartwheels. But I simply slunk back into the darkness and gnawed on what was left of the vermin. I tried not to let the whole thing piss me off. I knew I had to stay focused, that's why I had fought the urge to follow Kiera on the few occasions she had left her apartment, like I had followed her before. I kept telling myself that what she did in this world had nothing to do with me. And besides, I took no satisfaction in watching her with Sparky or watching Kiera cry herself to sleep at night. That was one thing I had found difficult to deal with. Why had Kiera been crying that night? Something bad had happened and I wondered if Kiera's and Sparky's relationship was as tight as it had first appeared. I kept trying to tell myself to let go – to forget about the Kiera living across the street and to concentrate on the task in hand. I hadn't left the alleyway once, not since the night I had gone after Kiera, and so far there had been no sign of the photographer. How long would it take for him to put in an appearance? For how many more days and nights could I risk hiding out in the street before I got arrested on suspicion of being a pervert? Maybe a night or two in the police cells would be a good thing – at least I'd get hot food and a decent night's sleep. Sleeping was hard, not only because it had pretty much rained since coming back, and the ground was covered in puddles, I just couldn't afford to sleep. Knowing my luck, the moment I got some shut-eye, the photographer would put in an appearance and the whole mission would've been just a waste of time. Instead of discovering the identity of the photographer, the only thing I would have discovered is that the woman I loved most in the world was dating a freaking werewolf – in this world, at least!

It was early evening on the third night and I was struggling to keep my eyes open. I had run out of cigarettes and the cravings were bad. The nicotine did help to ease my need for the red stuff. I think I'd scared most of the vermin away so there was nothing else to eat. I slid down the alley wall and wrapped my coat about myself as tightly as I could. Cupping my hands together, I brought them up to my lips and blew warm air from my lungs across them. They felt like a pack of frozen fish fingers. I leant forward and rested my forehead against my hands. I closed my eyes, and rocked forward, any movement to try and keep myself warm. With my eyes shut tight, I wished for a cigarette.

"Please hurry up and deliver the photograph," I whispered. I didn't know for how much longer I could take the cold and lack of sleep.

"What photograph?" I heard someone suddenly say.

I opened my eyes to see Kiera standing in the opening of the alleyway. She was holding an open umbrella and the rain was drumming off the top of it. She looked real pretty in the pale blue top she was wearing with black jeans and trainers.

"Huh?" I said, surprised at seeing her standing there looking down at me. I scrambled to my feet.

"What are you doing in the alleyway, Potter?" she scowled.

"I was just passing," I mumbled, unable to think of a better excuse so quickly.

"Liar," she said, staring out at me from beneath the umbrella. "You've been watching my apartment for the last three days."

"No I haven't," I lied. "I've only been here a few minutes. I ducked into the alleyway to keep out of the rain."

"And smoked several packs of cigarettes?" she said, looking down at the hundred or so scattered cigarette ends floating in the puddles.

"They're not all mine," I said.

"I've seen you, Potter," Kiera said. "If you're going to do a stakeout at night, don't smoke. The ends of your countless cigarettes have been winking on and off like a set of Christmas tree lights."

"You've known I've been hiding out in this rat-infested alleyway in the pissing rain for the last few days and you haven't so much as even brought me out a hot cup of coffee?" I sighed in disbelief.

"So you have been spying on me?" she asked, her voice now sounding angry.

"I haven't been spying on you..." I started.

"What have you been doing then?" she demanded.

"It's not what you think," I said, looking straight back at her.

"You don't even want to know what I'm thinking right at this moment," she seethed.

"Go on, surprise me," I muttered, patting my coat pockets down just in case there was a cigarette hiding someplace.

"You're working for the wolves," she said, accusing.

"What?" I gasped. "Is this some kind of a joke?"

"Don't lie to me," she shot back. "I know you're working with them."

"Not me, sweet-cheeks," I said, still patting my pockets.

"Don't call me that!" she barked. "You don't get to say stuff like that to me anymore."

"So who does get to say stuff like that to you now?" I shot back, forgetting that I was now talking to the Kiera Hudson of this world and not my own. "Is Sparky the one who gets to say stuff like that these days?"

"Oh, my God," Kiera said, staring at me. "So this is what it's all about."

"What's what about?" I said, shaking my head at her.

"Perhaps I was wrong," Kiera gasped. "Perhaps you're not working with the wolves and the reason you've been watching me is because you thought you could stroll back into my life like nothing had happened and climb straight back into my bed. You couldn't believe that I threw you out the other night. Your bruised ego told you that you couldn't possibly be the problem, so you thought that there might be someone else in my life – someone else who had taken your place in my bed."

"And is there?" I asked before thinking.

"That is none of your business," she quite rightly reminded me.

It was none of my business; I kept trying to tell myself.

A heavy silence hung between us, which was filled by the rain splashing into the puddles at my feet and bouncing off Kiera's umbrella.

"So where are you living these days?" she eventually asked, her voice cooling a bit.

"Nowhere," I shrugged, looking down at the puddles. "Why do you care?"

"You look filthy dirty," she said. "Like you haven't shaved or showered in days. Are you homeless, Potter? Are you in some kind of trouble? Is that why you've come back?"

I looked up at her as she peered at me from beneath the umbrella. "I should go," I said.

"Go where?" she asked, her voice softer somehow.

"Back to nowhere, I guess," I said, brushing past her.

I stepped out of the alleyway and onto the pavement. The wind blew hard and cold about me and I shivered, pulling up the collar of my coat about my throat. I walked away without looking back at her.

"What about that coffee?" Kiera called after me.

I stopped, my heart beginning to race.

Don't get involved with the Kiera Hudson from the pushed world, I heard Lilly Blu warn me.

"I think I still have a couple of old packs of cigarettes

someplace," Kiera said. "You left them behind when you ran out…"

I turned to face her and she stopped mid-sentence. We stood there in the rain staring at each other. It wasn't a cigarette I wanted – it was Kiera I wanted. My Kiera or not – I just wanted to be held by her.

"You don't smoke," I looked at her. "Why did you keep them?"

"I dunno," she said, looking straight back at me, then quickly added, "so do you want that coffee or not? I'm not going to ask again."

Kiera turned her back on me and headed across the road. She stepped back into the apartment block, leaving the front door open behind her.

Should I stay or should I go?

The Kiera from this world had seen me now – she knew I had been watching her. My cover had been blown. I was more likely to catch this photographer if I stuck close with Kiera, I tried to convince myself. As long as I didn't change anything in this world, I should be okay. Right? I was only going to have a coffee with Kiera, that's all. What changes could I make to her life by having coffee?

I looked back at the alley where I'd spent the last few days and nights freezing my nuts off. In the dark, narrow mouth of the alleyway stood the little girl. Her dark hair was plastered to her pale face with rain. Her dress was soaked through. She looked at me and waved her thin, white hand. I turned my back on her and crossed the road towards Kiera's apartment block. I closed the door behind me.

I climbed the short flight of stairs to Kiera's apartment. Her front door was open. I stepped inside and shut the door. Kiera walked out of her bedroom carrying a small pile of clean clothes and a towel, handing them to me. Placed on top were two packs of cigarettes. I thumbed through the clothes.

"You left those, too, when you left," she said, turning and

heading towards the kitchen. "Take a shower while I make some coffee."

I went to the bathroom and closed the door. I peeled of my filthy clothes and switched on the shower. Water hissed from the showerhead, coils of steam billowing up and covering the small window and mirror with condensation. Instead of getting under the water, I sat on the edge of the bath and lit a cigarette. I drew in a lungful of thick, grey smoke and began to cry. I wasn't sure why, but my body shook as the running water drowned out the sound of my sobs. I leant forward and covered my eyes with my forearm as smoke trailed up from the tip of the cigarette dangling between my fingers. I felt ashamed for how I had treated Kiera. I had treated her bad not only in my world, but in this *pushed* world, too. In both worlds she had been hurt by me – yet, in both she still showed me kindness and love. I had obviously hurt her very badly in this world – run out on her and left her all alone – yet she had come to me in the freezing cold and taken me in. She was a friend like no other and I just kept hurting her. Kiera deserved better – they *both* did. And deep down I knew why I was crying, because it was me Kiera had been crying over the other night. However much I wanted to tell myself it had been Sparky who had hurt her – I knew in my selfish heart it had been me. What kind of man reduces the woman he loves to tears like that? Not a good man – that was for sure. I hated Jack Seth for the pain and hurt he had caused people – but if I were honest with myself – I was no better than him. In fact, I was probably worse. Jack had never claimed to have loved any of his victims. Yet I claimed to love Kiera but had done nothing but hurt her. That's what I was ashamed of.

I wiped away my tears with my arm. I ditched the cigarette into the toilet bowl and flushed it away. Standing beneath the running water, I washed the dirt and grime from my body. The water was hot and it melted the chill that had taken hold of my bones. After towelling myself dry, I put on the other Potter's clothes. Wearing a clean pair of black jeans and T-shirt, I left the bathroom.

Kiera was sitting in her chair by the window and looking out into the dark. She held a mug of coffee in her hands. There was another on the table beside her. I crossed the room and picked it up. Kiera continued to stare out of the window.

I raised the mug of coffee to my lips, then stopped. "I'm sorry," I whispered.

"For what?" she whispered back, still staring blankly out of the window.

"For all the hurt I've ever caused you," I said.

"It's a bit late for sorry," Kiera said, getting up from her chair and heading for her bedroom door. "You can stay tonight, if you really have *nowhere* else to stay. You'll have to make do with the armchair."

Kiera turned away again, stepping into her bedroom. Before she closed the door, I said, "Hey, Kiera."

"What?" she said, without looking back.

"I don't deserve a friend like you," I said.

She closed the door, leaving me alone once again.

Chapter Nineteen

Jack

I crouched beside the trees in the woods all that night. It was bitterly cold – too cold to sleep. I dozed a little, but mostly I was awake. The photographer didn't come and I still suspected that he or she wouldn't – not until Melody Rose died. How the girl ended up dead – I still had no idea. Potter hadn't said. As the wind whipped and howled through the trees, sending up gusts of leaves into the air, I wished now that I had known. That piece of information might have given me some idea as to how long I would have to follow Isi-*bore* and Melody *Doze* about for. They weren't the most exciting of people to tag along behind.

But maybe their lives weren't as dull as I'd first thought. Why had they hidden in that wardrobe? That had taken some guts. And the look on Melody's face as they had come tumbling out of it – I couldn't get that look out of my head. I had seen that expression so many times before. It was the look of sheer fear. But what did she have to be so scared of? Her mother? She seemed harmless enough. By the way she dressed, the little church, and all the praying that was going on, the mother struck me as one of those God-fearing types. Not too much to be scared of there.

So when Isidor popped his head above ground again the following morning, I decided to follow him once more. He had an anxious look on his face as he made his way back through the woods and towards the lake. His look of anxiousness soon turned to one of relief on finding the girl waiting for him on the shore. She was dressed in the same dull clothes, but today she carried a rucksack over her shoulder. I knew then he had probably lain awake all night deep within The Hollows fretting about the girl he so obviously loved. Isi-bore had pleaded with the girl to go with him the night before. It was like he suspected she was in some kind of danger.

Together they walked along the shoreline. I wanted to stay as close as possible so as to hear what it was they talked so deeply about. Crouching low, I shook all over, releasing my coat of black fur, claws, long snout, and bushy tail. I slinked along in the shadows of the trees and the undergrowth which surrounded them.

"You won't ever tell anyone what you saw and heard at my house, will you?" the girl asked him, her voice full of dread.

"I can't believe you have to ask me that," Isi-bore said, sounding hurt by her lack of faith in him.

What had the boy seen and heard that the girl could worry so much about, I wondered.

Secrets, perhaps? I knew all about them. I'd grown up in a house with a mother who had kept plenty of them.

"I know I can trust you, but I would hate for anybody else to find out," I heard Melody say as I crept along just feet away, my wolf shaped body low, belly brushing against the leaves and undergrowth.

"Well they won't find out from me. I promise," Isi-bore tried to assure her.

They reached the mouth of their secret camp, but instead of sneaking inside like they had the day before, they sat on the sand, which led down to the black coloured waters of the lake.

Still disguised as a wolf, my black fur offered me a certain amount of camouflage on the edge of the dark woods, I watched Melody place the rucksack on the ground. She took an old-fashioned looking radio from it.

"I thought we could listen to some music," the girl said, smiling that crooked smile at Isi-bore.

The boy didn't say anything; he just kinda stared back at her with that dumb look on his face. Melody switched the radio on. There was a hissing of static as she turned the silver dial on top of the radio. A song started to play. It was a song I hadn't heard for many years. I sat and listened from beneath a nearby tree as Melody started to sing along with David Bowie as he sung *Heroes*.

The music almost seemed to animate Melody – as if bringing her to life somehow. She sat next to Isi-bore in the sand, singing along to the music and clicking her fingers. She looked happy, and for once her smile didn't look so bad. I crouched low, my tail twitching from side to side and listened to the words of the song, and I couldn't help but think of me and my younger brother – when we were younger – before we had become killers. I guess if our lives had turned out different – Nik and I could have been heroes too, instead of monsters.

"Are you wearing makeup?" I suddenly heard Isi-bore ask Melody. He sounded kinda shocked by this.

"Yeah, do you like it?" Melody smiled back at him.

"What would your mother say?" Isi-bore asked.

The mother thing again, I noticed.

"She won't find out," Melody said and I watched her take a lipstick from her bag. She sat and smeared it over her lips.

"Where did you get the makeup from?" Isi-bore asked.

Does it matter where she got the fucking lipstick from? I sighed. You're meant to be telling the girl how goddamn freaking hot she looks. She wants you to tell her she looks beautiful, you dumb-fuck.

"From a shop," Melody told him, pointing down at the pouch in her apron. Then, she added, "Comes in real handy for slipping things in."

"You stole that makeup?" Isi-bore asked wide-eyed as if she had just confessed to spraying a bank full of customers with machine gunfire then running off with the loot.

It's a fucking lipstick! Get a grip, I felt like hollering at him.

"Just like you and the library book," Melody winked at him.

Well, well, well! I smiled slyly to myself. The boy's a thief, too. Stealing from a library, huh? But then again, that just showed what a complete and utter fucking retard the kid was. I'd never heard of someone who can't read stealing a freaking book before. What was the fucking point in that!

"Speaking of books," Melody cut in. "I've got something for you."

Not more reading! Surely not! I was just starting to like her too, now she had to go and spoil things.

The girl pulled what looked like a comic book from her bag.

"Why have you got me a book?" Isi-bore asked her.

Yeah, why bring the kid a book? That's a bit fucking cruel. I was beginning to like her again.

"You know I can't read," Isi-bore reminded her.

"But I can," Melody smiled. "I'm gonna teach you."

Fuck me, this just gets worse and worse, I sighed, rolling onto my side in the leaves. This is going to be a long fucking day. I lay on my side and listened to Melody explain to the dumb-fuck that the comic book was called the Incredible Hulk. Why he couldn't figure that out himself by looking at the big green monster on the front, beat the shit out of me.

"What's it about?" he asked, and I cringed.

He's got to be taking the piss. No one can be that fucking thick.

"This dude – his name is Bruce Banner but he leads a secret life," Melody started to explain. "Everyone thinks he's like, a regular guy, but really he's a monster. He can't tell anyone, because if people find out they..."

"Would capture him, put him in a cage, then open him up to see how he worked," Isi-bore cut in.

They'd stick you in fucking jail – like that sonofabitch Murphy did to me, I thought as I listened to Melody explain the story to numb-nuts.

"People don't like *different*, do they?" I heard Isi-bore say.

No, people certainly don't like different, you've got that right at least, I thought.

I hid amongst the trees, as Melody sat just a few feet away and helped Isi-bore to read. At times I was so bored, I snuck away before I lost the will to live. I found a tree to take a leak against, then headed back, just to make sure that they hadn't wandered off and I missed the next exciting episode in their adventurous lives.

For the next few days they came back to the same spot, Melody sat patiently beside Isi-bore as she taught him how to read the words in the books she brought each day to the lake. The radio played in the background, and each time Heroes came on,

Melody would sit and sing along, clicking her fingers and swaying from side to side. Once the song faded out at the end, Melody would go back to tracing her fingers under the words that Isi-bore was quickly learning to read and understand. And it was as I stood sloped against a tree and spied on them sitting together, I remembered how Father Paul had sat patiently with me as a boy, about the same age as Isi-bore, as I taught myself to paint and draw. Just like Melody sat patiently with Isidor, Father Paul had sat with me, teaching me how to use the watercolour paints he had bought me as a present.

"It reminds you, doesn't it?" a voice said from beside me.

I glanced right to see the bride standing just a few feet away.

"Is Isidor so different to what you were like at his age?" she asked, her virgin white dress flapping gently as she spoke from behind it.

"That fuck-wit is nothing like me," I barked under my breath at her.

"Perhaps you're right," she said, turning away, her long, white dress trailing out behind her in the dead leaves and mulch. "You're nothing like the boy Isidor."

I looked away, I wasn't in the mood to play fucking word games with a figment of my own imagination.

The girl didn't always come to the lake each day like Isi-bore did. I didn't want to spend my days watching him. I had started to feel uncomfortable around him. I wasn't sure why – but there was something. So instead, I followed the girl when she wasn't with Isi-bore. I didn't know where she went or what she did, so I headed for her home. It was still light when I arrived, guessing that she would be there as night drew in. I watched the house from the shelter of the trees that grew along each side of the narrow lane, leading to the house. Her mother's car wasn't out front and I wondered if Melody was home alone. It was still too light for me to climb the front of the house like I had done a few nights before, so I slipped from my hiding place and crept around the side of the house to where the basement was. I dropped over the stone wall and knelt down so I could peer into the small basement window. I pressed my nose against the dirty sheet of glass. It was dark inside and I couldn't see very much at all, apart from the outline of the huge cross I'd seen before. I knelt back from the window and wondered if I could get it open, whether I might be able to squeeze through into the basement. I was tall and incredibly scrawny, so I might just fit through. Releasing my claws, I hooked one finger and ran the sharp nail around the seal. I cut away some of the wooden window frame, making a big enough gap to slide my fingers through. I could feel the latch on the other side of the window. Glancing over the wall just to make sure that I wouldn't be disturbed, I knocked the catch free with one of my long fingernails. Lifting the window open, my heart started to race at the rush of memories in which I had broken into the homes and apartments of so many women before.

Make sure you don't hurt one single petal on any beautiful roses you might find, I heard Noah whisper in my ear.

I blocked his voice out of my mind. Crouching so I was flat against the ground, I eased one of my rake-thin arms through the open window followed by my head and shoulders. I dangled over the edge of the window and slid down into the basement. Reaching out with my long arms, I braced my fall so as not to crack my head against the grey slate basement floor. I stood up and brushed the dust from my jeans and the elbows of my coat. After closing the window again, I started to check out the basement come makeshift chapel. The air stank of wax and incense. I screwed up my nose and sneezed. I stood in the semi darkness and looked up. I was waiting to hear any movement from above. If Melody was home, then surely she would have heard me sneeze. When I was quite sure I was alone, I made my way to the altar at the front of the chapel. I stopped before the giant cross and noticed that someone had placed a small wooden box before it. It was the size of a crate and was big enough to stand on. I was about to inspect the chapel further, when I heard the sound of a car approaching along the dirt road leading to the house.

Mother's home, I thought to myself, heading back across the chapel to the window. I pushed it open with my fingertips, a rush of air snaking inside and blowing my wispy fringe from my narrow brow. Through the open window I heard the sound of someone cry out.

"I'm sorry, Momma!"

It was Melody's voice I heard.

"Get inside and go to the chapel," her mother hissed.

Knowing that I would soon have company, I tried to scramble back up the wall to the window. I pushed the window open and poked one of my arms through. Even on tiptoe I couldn't lever myself up and out of the window. I looked back at the box on the floor before the cross. The sound of a bolt being slid sharply back echoed like gunfire from above. This was followed by the sound of footfalls on the wooden stairs leading down into the chapel. Knowing that I wasn't going to escape, I slunk back into the corner of the room, where a statue of the Sacred Heart stood. I pressed myself flat against the wall and hid behind it.

There was a sharp scratching sound, then a flame. It lit up Melody's mother's face in the gloom like a Halloween pumpkin. She lit several candles at the feet of the Madonna statue on the opposite side of the chapel from where I was hiding.

"I'm sorry, Momma," I heard Melody sob.

I peered around the edge of the statue to see Melody cowering before the huge cross in front of the altar

"Slut!" her mother screamed, her breath blowing out the match that was burning down between her fingers. "Filthy little whore! You disgust me!"

"I'm sorry, Momma," Melody sobbed through fear more than sadness.

"And you disgust the mother of Christ! Look at her! Look at her!" the mad-looking woman screeched, eyes bulging in their sockets as she forced Melody to stand before the statue of the Madonna. "Does she wear nail varnish? Does she wear lipstick? Does she dress up like a filthy-looking whore?"

"No, Momma," Melody cried, lowering her head so she didn't

have to look at the statue which stared blankly down at her.

Raising the flat of her hand, the woman smacked her daughter in the face. There was an audible *crack* as Melody's head snapped backwards, her bonnet falling free and hanging down her back, trapped by the black cord around her throat. The woman then made a fist as she grabbed Melody by the hair.

"Women who look like whores attract the devil," she breathed into Melody's face. "Do you want the devil to come for you?"

"No, Momma," Melody sobbed, turning her head to the side as if her mother's breath stank.

"Because the devil came to me once," the woman hissed onto her daughter's face. "He came and took me, put his seed inside of me – he put *you* inside of me."

"I'm sorry, Momma... forgive me..." Melody cried out.

"It's not my forgiveness you need," her mother screeched into Melody's upturned face. "It is the Lord's forgiveness you must seek."

Melody cried out and threw her hands to her head as her mother grabbed her daughter by the hair, pulling her towards the altar. "Over the box," her mother seethed, forcing her daughter to bend over.

"No, Momma," Melody sobbed hysterically as if knowing what was coming.

To watch what was happening from my hiding place behind the statue I couldn't help but be reminded of the relationship I'd had with my own mother. Her room had been adorned with statues of the Elders, just like this room had been decorated with figurines. I remembered my mother catching me drawing on the garden wall with chalk and she had forced me to take my clothes off and stand in the cold while I prayed for forgiveness from the Elders.

You're a sinner and you must repent! Now get on your knees and pray to the Elders. I heard my mother's voice as if she were standing beside me.

I stood behind the statue and covered my ears with my

hands, and in my heart I didn't know if I were blocking out the sound of my own mother's voice, or that of Melody's momma.

The woman forced Melody into a kneeling position over the box before the huge cross. Melody's momma had that crazy, wide-eyed look that my own mother had in her eyes when she had punished me for such minor indiscretions.

She hitched up the girl's skirt, revealing the backs of her bare legs. Melody tried to pull her dress down again and I understood why. I remembered those feelings of embarrassment I had felt as my own mother had made me strip in the garden. I hadn't wanted her to see me like that – it had been humiliating. And I felt Melody's humiliation now. I closed my eyes over the tears that stung in them. The urge to leap from behind my hiding place and rip Melody's mother's fucking head clean off was almost unbearable. But I remembered what Lilly Blu had said – she had told me not to get involved – not to change anything in this world. The woman who was now torturing her daughter before me wasn't my mother, and I had to find a way of letting go.

So however much I wanted to kill that fucking bitch, just like I had killed my own mother, I had to stay hidden as Melody's momma took what looked like a small leather whip from the pouch on the front of her apron. With one hand gripping the back of Melody's neck, forcing her into a kneeling position, the woman whipped the back of her daughter's legs.

With each deafening crack of the whip lashing across Melody's skin, I flinched in the darkness behind the statue. Melody screamed in agony, her young voice sounding shrill. I placed my hands over my ears. Melody's cries reminded me too much of my sister Kara's screams as she died in my arms all those years ago. The sound of Melody's screams and my own memories were un-fucking-bearable. I rocked forward, the sound of my weeping, drowned out by the sound of the whipping being given to Melody.

When Melody was unable to scream no more, her mother stopped. The woman sagged backwards, gasping for breath. The exertion of whipping her daughter had obviously exhausted her.

Panting, she wiped the sweat from her wrinkled brow. Melody dropped to the ground like a broken doll.

"Get out of here," her momma breathed.

Melody tried to stand, then dropped to the floor again.

"Get out," the woman hissed, still struggling to catch her breath.

I watched Melody pull herself up onto her hands and knees and crawl away from her mother like some kind of beaten animal. I turned around and faced the wall, not only because I couldn't bear to watch any more, but the smell of blood running from the cuts crisscrossing the backs of Melody's legs was driving me half insane with hunger and lust. I heard the sound of Melody limping and falling as she made her way up the stairs and out of the makeshift chapel.

"I will beat the beast out of that child," I heard the mother say. She was so close now, I feared that I had been discovered and she was talking to me.

I glanced back over my shoulder to discover the woman now standing before the statue I was hiding behind. She gazed up into the Sacred Heart's face – a look of ecstasy gleaming in her eyes.

"The devil tempted me once," she whispered up into the statue's face. "I won't let him tempt my daughter."

She then turned away, blew out the candle, and left the chapel. No sooner had she bolted the door closed at the top of the stairs, I raced from my hiding place and snatched up the box. I placed it against the wall beneath the window, and scrambled from the chapel.

It was almost dark and I ran towards the trees lining the road. I looked back at the house, still fighting the urge to go back and kill the woman living inside of it. The front door opened. Melody appeared on the porch, and over her shoulder she carried the rucksack I had seen her with before. Had she plucked up the courage to leave the sick bitch behind? Had she decided to take Isidor up on his offer and run away with him?

I watched her stagger down the front path. She winced at every footstep she took. Melody bit into her lower lip, fighting the urge to scream in pain as she limped past me. Hoping that she had decided to leave and find peace with Isidor, just like I had found sanctuary with Father Paul, I followed her. As the last rays of sunlight faded in the sky over the lake, Melody reached the shore. Isi-bore was sitting before the dark waters, crouched over what looked like some kind of notebook. He looked up to see Melody approach him.

From the safety of the woods, I watched Melody limp forwards, dragging her rucksack behind her in the sand. She took a folded piece of white paper from her apron. Isi-bore jumped up and ran towards her. I watched as he took the rucksack from Melody.

"What's that?" he asked, looking at the piece of paper held in her hand.

"A copy of the school dress code," Melody said, screwing up the piece of paper and throwing it away.

"What's happened?" I heard Isi-bore ask.

"A good whipping, that's what happened," Melody said, stumbling forward into Isi-bore's arms.

He helped Melody to sit down, and she cried out in pain. "It's the back of my legs, cut to ribbons they are."

"Your mum whipped you, didn't she?" Isi-bore said, a sudden look of anger falling over his face.

Melody nodded.

"Why did she do it?" the boy asked, sitting beside her.

"A teacher noticed that I was wearing nail varnish," Melody explained. "I forgot that I was wearing it. You're not allowed to wear it at school. It's not a big deal, really, but they called my mum. She came up to the school and took me home. She said the usual crap about how the devil was tempting me – and that only whores wear makeup."

"Where is she now?" Isi-bore snapped.

Good boy! I thought. Go on – show some fucking backbone for once. Go round and rip that fucking bitch's heart out.

"She's praying for me," Melody told him. "Isidor, are you all right?"

"No," he said, staggering away from her. "I've got to go."

"Go where?" Melody asked, looking hurt. "I need you."

"Sorry," Isi-bore almost seemed to gag, then turned and fled.

He is actually going to man-up and kill that bitch!

Leaving Melody alone on the shore, I went after Isi-bore as he raced away through the woods. I wanted to see if he really would kill Melody's mother. I couldn't believe Isi-bore could. And I was right. I soon realised he wasn't racing back towards town and Melody's home, but heading back towards the grate in the ground which would take him back to The Hollows.

I went after him, and as he fled, two giant black wings sprung from beneath his arms. He slid face-first into the dirt and yanked open the grate. Without looking back, he disappeared back beneath ground. I stood and looked down into the hole. Isi-bore had gone. I kicked the grate shut with my boot. Turning around, I saw the bride watching me from behind a tree.

"You were wrong," I whispered.

"About what?" she asked from behind her veil.

"Me and the boy. I am nothing like him. If anyone had treated the person I loved so badly, I would have ripped her fucking spine out," I said through gritted teeth, then walked away.

I reached the shore to find that Melody had gone. Where? Back home, I guessed. Where else did she have to go? From the corner of my eye, I saw the crumpled piece of paper that the girl had thrown away. I picked it up. It was a list of the school uniform rules and a letter to Melody's mother. The letter explained how Melody had broken the school rules. It had been signed by the deputy head teacher. Her name was Mrs. Last.

That would be the *last* fucking letter she would be sending home to Melody's mother, or anybody else's for that matter, I smiled, tossing the piece of paper back into the sand.

With my claws already out, I headed back towards town in search of Mrs. Last. I planned on spending the rest of the night having some fun with her.

Chapter Twenty

Potter

I slept little. I hoped I would have slept more. It wasn't that Kiera's armchair was uncomfortable – it was way better then standing out in the freezing cold alleyway. What kept me awake was the hundreds and hundreds of newspaper clippings Kiera had tacked to the walls of her living room. My Kiera had often done the same thing, and I could remember that she had done exactly the same during our short stay at Hallowed Manor on our arrival into this *pushed* world. Perhaps both Kieras' had some slight compulsive behavioural disorder? But in my heart I knew that wasn't true. The Kiera I knew and loved only did this kinda shit when she was looking for someone or something.

In the glow of the small lamp, I eventually got up out of the armchair and began to inspect the newspaper cuttings. Pretty much all of them were reports about killings and murders that had taken place or about people who had suddenly gone missing. As I worked away around the room, I noticed other articles too that were about people who claimed to have lived past lives – different kind of lives. There were so many clippings that it seemed quite a phenomenon in this *pushed* world. Was this a result of Noah sitting in his ticket booth, punching out all those tickets? I wondered. Was the fact that so many people appeared to be convinced they had lived some kind of an alternate life the result of all the cracks Noah and Lilly had been making? But why was Kiera so interested in these news reports? Had she started to remember too? I continued to check out the hundreds of articles until my heart suddenly stopped dead in my chest. There was a face I recognised peering back at me from all of those black and white newspaper cuttings. It was Kayla's face looking back at me. Slowly, I reached out and unpinned the article, which reported how Kayla and her brother, Isidor, had been butchered by their father, Doctor Hunt on the Cumbrian mountainside. Just like Murphy had told me, the report stated that Doctor Hunt had been delusional and had believed both his children were winged creatures who had come from a world beneath ground.

"Interesting, don't you think?" I heard someone ask.

I spun around to find Kiera standing in her bedroom doorway. She wore a crimson coloured dressing gown that was fastened about her waist. She stepped into the room, and I caught a glimpse of her milky coloured thigh as she came towards me. I looked quickly away.

"Did you know this girl?" I asked tentatively, holding the newspaper clipping between my fingers.

"No," Kiera said with a swift shake of her head and looked down at the picture. "But..." she trailed off.

"But what?" I asked, my heart speeding up.

"I don't know," she sighed, turning away.

"Why did you tear this from the newspaper and keep it if you don't know the girl in the picture?"

"Her story interested me, that's all," she said, going to the window and looking down at the street.

The first rays of morning light were creeping over the roofs of the houses in the street, and they showered Kiera's pale face with a soft pink glow. Remembering that Lilly had said there was a message for Murphy on the back of this newspaper clipping, I slid it into my pocket to read later.

"What was so interesting about it? People get killed all the time," I asked, sensing now that perhaps this Kiera had started to make a connection with her other life.

"The girl and her brother, Isidor, were murdered, because their father believed they were winged creatures," she said, still looking out of the window. "He was so convinced his two children had giant black wings hidden inside them, he cut them open and removed their spines. Don't you think that's a bit odd?" Now she turned to look directly at me.

"Odd?" I shrugged, trying to dismiss her comments. "The guy who did that to his kids sounds like a fucking whack-job."

"Maybe his beliefs weren't so crazy after all," Kiera said. "Perhaps he was right."

"You've got to be kidding me, right?" I half-smiled at her. "Winged creatures from beneath ground. You'll be trying to tell me the Smurfs are real next."

"Smurfs?" she frowned.

Did they have Smurf cartoons in the *pushed* world? I didn't know and besides, who gave a crap? "Look, forget the Smurfs. My point is that this whole thing about creatures with wings is just a bunch of bullshit."

"Is it?" Kiera said, turning her back towards me and dropping her dressing gown halfway down her back. "What are these then?"

I looked at Kiera's back and gasped at the sight of the three bony-looking lumps beneath the skin covering each of her shoulder blades.

"Horrible, aren't they?" she whispered, lowering her head as if in shame. She pulled the dressing gown back up to cover her shoulders.

"I don't know what to say," I mumbled, and I really didn't. What could I say? Should I tell her the truth about everything? No I couldn't do that. I couldn't afford for Kiera to remember anything. Lilly had said that would be really dangerous. I didn't know exactly what Lilly had meant by her warning – but should this Kiera remember, could that be dangerous for my Kiera? I couldn't risk that. "Look, I think I should go…"

"Running out on me again, Potter?" Kiera whispered, turning to look at me. I could see the tears slowly rolling down the length of her beautiful face.

"No… I'm…" I started.

"I sicken you, don't I?" she said, her lower lip trembling. "I'm hideous… a freak."

How could I let her stand before me and cry believing that she was a freak, when I truly knew what she was? But I couldn't tell her the truth, either. I crossed the room and took her gently in my arms. She didn't push me away, but buried her face against my chest and sobbed.

Holding her felt no different than holding my Kiera.

"But she's not *your* Kiera," a voice whispered.

I glanced sideways to see the little girl with the long, dark hair and red dress standing in the open doorway of Kiera's bedroom. I looked away because I knew what she said was true. But what could I do? Walk out on her again?

"But that wasn't you," I heard the little girl whisper as if she were able to hear my thoughts.

I couldn't walk out – not now, despite knowing in my heart that I should. Glancing back at the bedroom door, I could see that the little girl had gone again. Kiera continued to sob in my arms as I held her. I knew she was scared – I could feel her fear.

"You're not a freak," I whispered in her ear.

"What am I then?" she asked, easing herself back so she could look up into my eyes.

Whether this was my Kiera or not – I couldn't lie to her. Lying would get me *nowhere*. Kiera had taught me that. I wanted to tell her the truth. I wanted to show her my wings – to prove to her she wasn't alone like she believed she was.

"Kiera... you're... a..." I started, then stopped as the song *Just the way you are* by Bruno Mars started to play from somewhere in the apartment.

The last time I'd heard that song was when Kiera and I had made love in the bunker beneath the hangar on the outskirts of Wasp Water. Kiera slipped from my arms.

"That's my phone," she whispered, wiping the tears from her cheeks with the balls of her hands. She crossed the room, and picking her jacket up from off the floor, Kiera fished her phone from one of the pockets.

"Kiera," she said into the phone, trying to make her voice so steady to hide the fact she had just been crying. "Hey, John."

Sparky? I guessed.

"Really?" she breathed. "What, at this time of the morning?"

She paused and listened.

"Where did this happen?" she asked. "Okay. I'm on my way."

She pressed the disconnect button.

"Sparky?" I cocked an eyebrow at her.

"Yes," she nodded, heading for the bathroom. "I've got to go."

"Go where?" I asked.

"A youth has been struck and killed by a train on a desolate stretch of track a few miles from here," she said, looking back at me.

"So what's that got to do with you?" I asked, taking a cigarette from one of the packets she had given me and lighting it.

"I'm a cop, remember?" she half-smiled.

"What I meant was, why have you got to go? You're not even on duty. Are you like the only cop left in this town?" I said.

"Might as well be," she shrugged. "Most of the cops are wolves and they don't really care about what happens to humans. It's really just down to me and Spar... John... to police this place."

"So why doesn't *Sparky*, go and deal with the kid under the train?" I asked, blowing smoke from the side of my mouth.

"He said he's got another job he's dealing with, a domestic or something," Kiera explained.

"So you're going alone?" I asked.

"I've got used to being alone, remember?" she said right back, stepping into the bathroom.

Before she closed the door fully, I said, "I'm going to come with you."

"Why?" she asked, peering through the gap in the door at me.

"I'm a cop, too, remember?" I said.

Within ten minutes of receiving the call from Sparky, I was sitting in Kiera's tiny little red car as she drove towards the scene of the incident. It was such a tight fit in the Mini that my knees were drawn up so far that my chin nearly rested against them.

The early morning sky had turned overcast and it looked like we were gonna get more rain. Looking at Kiera, I said as casually as possible, "So why that particular song?"

"What song?" Kiera asked, switching on the windscreen wipers at the first splashes of rain.

"The one you use as a ringtone," I reminded her.

"I like it. Why?" she asked.

"No reason," I lied.

We sat in silence; I guess neither of us knowing what to say. Then turning to look at her, I said, "Why did you show me those... those... lumps on your back?"

"Because the thought of them scares me," she said, her eyes fixed on the road ahead. "I needed to show someone."

"What does Sparky think they are?" I asked, wondering if I was now pushing my luck.

"He hasn't seen them," Kiera said.

"No?" I said, trying to hide my surprise. "But I thought you two were..."

"What?" she asked, shooting me a sideways glance.

"You know."

"No, I don't know, Potter," she said, looking back at the rain-slicked country road we were now heading along.

"I thought you two were having jiggy-jiggy." I didn't know how to say it.

"What's jiggy-jiggy?" she asked.

I looked at her. "You know... a bit of humpty-dumpty..." I then saw the faintest of smiles tugging at the corners of her lips. "If you're gonna take the piss, I won't bother talking to you. You know exactly what I mean."

"If you must know," she said, slowing the car to navigate a tight bend in the winding road, "me and John are just good friends."

"Really?" I asked, trying to mask my delight at this news. "But I thought you two were..."

"Having humpty-dumpty, as you so eloquently described it?" she cut in.

"Well, yeah," I said.

"So now you know," she said.

I looked out of the window again and tried to hide my grin.

There was another long silence, only filled by the squeaking sound of the wipers driving away the rain.

This time Kiera spoke first. "So have you had jiggy-jiggy with anyone else since... since you left?" she asked, unable to bring herself to look at me.

How did I answer that? There had been another... the other Kiera.

"No," I said. "There has only been you."

Was that really I lie? My brain was starting to ache.

"Okay," she said, that little smile tugging at the corner of her lips again.

Wanting to change the subject and unable to think of anything else to say, I said the first thing that came into my head. "So what do you think those lumps are?"

"My wings," she said.

"You're shitting me, right?" I asked, staring at her.

"Why couldn't they be?" she asked right back.

"Because people don't have wings, Kiera," I told her.

"Perhaps," she said, more to herself than to me.

How much did Kiera know? How much did she remember? Were her wings breaking through a result of the cracks Noah was making?

Kiera slowed the car to a stop and killed the engine. She pushed open the car door and climbed out and I followed. It was raining hard, and as Kiera headed through the puddles towards the train in the distance, mud splashed over her boots and up the hem of the jeans she was wearing. It was a freight train which had struck the victim. Its engine was long and black and pumped thick clouds of diesel into the overcast sky. I couldn't help but be reminded of the train that had carried me here. Wind blew across the open fields on either side of us, and I thrust my hands into my coat pockets.

We reached the train and the whole scene seemed surreal to me. I had seen a lot of dead people in my life – some of those I had killed myself – but it was bizarre to see the upper half of this teenage boy's torso sticking out from beneath the train, whilst one white hairy leg lay further along the track wearing only a black shoe and sock. But the most peculiar thing about the whole incident was that the kid under the train was wearing a rubber Maggot Frogskin mask. Maggot had replaced Mickey Mouse in this *pushed* world, I reminded myself.

I think Kiera saw the look of bewilderment on my face and said, "Why don't you go and speak with the driver."

"Sure," I said, turning away from the dead kid wearing the mask. I made my way along the tracks to the driver's cab. I knew the whole point was to find out from the driver what had happened. Was the death of the kid a deliberate act on behalf of the deceased, suicide for instance, or was he being pursued or was he pushed in front of the train? In which case the area would be declared a crime scene and a full murder enquiry launched. But if what Kiera said was right about the wolves masquerading as cops in the town, they probably wouldn't give a diddly shit about how the kid ended up dead under the train. To them it would just be another dead human.

I established pretty quickly from speaking to the distraught train driver that the kid had been standing by the tracks as he approached.

"I blew up on the horn to warn him that I was approaching, but he just waved at me, pulled on one of those cartoon rubber masks, and stepped in front of my train! In all my years, I have never seen anything like it," the driver said, trembling and upset.

I made my way back to Kiera, my boots crunching on the ballast, to find her pulling the mask from over the deceased's head. The rubber mask made a *squelching* sound as it peeled off the kid's face.

"The driver said the kid just stepped out in front of the train," I said.

"Freaking wolves," Kiera cursed under her breath.

"What's this got to do with the wolves?" I asked.

Instead of answering my question, she said, "C'mon, give me a hand to get him out from under the train."

We bent at the knees and began to pull the upper torso free from under the train. I couldn't get what Kiera had said about the wolves from my head. Had she used that *seeing* thing she did in my world to figure out a wolf had been involved in this kid's death?

"Come on, Potter, don't wimp out on me now. I need your help, these things are heavy."

"Sorry," I said, pushing the remark Kiera had made about the wolves from the front of my mind.

We had found some I.D. in the kid's wallet which had made identifying him easy. His name was John Baker and he had been sixteen years old. Once the ambulance crew that Kiera had summoned to the scene had left the mortuary with the remains of John Baker's body, we made our way to his home address to inform his relatives of his death.

We climbed from Kiera's car and made our way up to the front door of the small house. It looked more like a shack than someone's home. Before we'd had a chance to knock, the door was flung open by a woman in her early thirties, who had a chocolate-smeared toddler clutched to her chest.

Kiera produced her police badge from her coat pocket and showed the woman.

"Thank you for coming so quickly, officers," she said in a panic-stricken voice.

"Why do you think we're here?" Kiera asked her.

No one had informed this woman about the death of the boy, as far as we knew, that's why we were knocking on her door.

"The note! I've just found John's note – says he's gonna kill himself... so I called the police station..." She then stared into Kiera's eyes. The woman holding the child must have seen the sorrow in them.

"No! No! No! I don't want to hear it... Go away..." and she started to push the door closed on us.

Kiera quickly put her hand out and prevented the woman from closing the door. We quietly made our way into her home.

John Baker had been this woman's younger brother. He had managed to escape from one of those schools run by the wolves. The school had been called Ravenwood. We sat and listened as

Baker's sister told us how her brother hadn't been the same since returning from that school. Although he had managed to escape, he had suffered from nightmares since his return.

"He felt guilty, you see?" the woman said.

"Guilty, why?" Kiera asked.

"He left his best friend, Sam Brook, behind. They had grown up together."

I knew she was talking about Kayla's friend Sam. Was I surprised by this connection? Not really. I guessed it was the two worlds overlapping like Murphy had said.

John Baker's sister described how she had often found him sitting alone at night and crying.

"I begged him to tell me what had happened there," the woman sobbed. "But all I got was nonsense."

"What kind of nonsense?" Kiera asked, taking a notebook from her pocket.

"He spoke of a place he called the Rat House," she said. "He would wake at night screaming in fear. Kicking and thrashing out with his legs and yelling that the rats were going to eat him."

"Did he describe anything else?" Kiera asked, making notes.

"Not really," she said, shaking her head and wiping her tears away.

The toddler the woman had been holding now ran about the room saying over and over again, "Maggot Frogskin! Maggot Frogskin!" The kid stopped only to search through a toy box on the floor.

I looked back at the woman as she sat and tried to stop the flow of tears streaming from her bloodshot eyes.

"Did your brother ever tell you how he managed to escape the wolves without being matched?" Kiera asked over the sound of the kid chucking toys around the room.

"No," she said, then after some thought added, "I thought my brother had gone mad."

"Why?" Kiera asked.

"John told me that the teachers often checked the children's hands for missing fingers, and he'd heard rumours that some of the girls had their backs checked to see if they had wings."

Kiera shot me a look. I turned away and watched the kid.

"Mummy, Mummy! Maggot Frogskin?" the kid asked, patting his mother's knee.

"Charlie, I haven't seen your Maggot Frogskin mask. Go and see if it's in your room."

Hearing this, I got up and left the house. Standing alone outside, I lit a cigarette. It was then I understood the comment Kiera had made beside the tracks about the wolves. The kids they didn't destroy through matching with them killed themselves because the wolves haunted their nightmares forever more.

Chapter Twenty-One

Jack

Isi-bore didn't return above ground for a few days. Part of me was glad about that. I occupied myself during the day by tagging along behind Melody, and by night I visited Mrs. Last. She didn't like the shallow grave I had her buried in, but she eventually stopped screaming when her mouth became clogged with earth and dirt. I killed her on the third night when the cops started combing the woods I was holding out in. They wouldn't have caught me, but this was the world where the Vampyrus had taken it upon themselves to hunt down wolves like me. I didn't want any freaking bats snooping about. Anyway, Mrs. Last had bored me, unlike Melody. She had started to interest me. On the morning after the whipping her mother had given her, I followed the girl to a tattoo shop on the outskirts of town. It was called 'Red Ink.' I liked that. There was a bar across the street, so buying myself a beer or two, I spent a couple of lazy days sitting across the street and watching Melody come and go from the tattoo parlour. Now what would Momma say if she knew? I wondered with a wry smile. What would Isi-bore say? Perhaps that's how he came about his own tattoos – the black flames that scorched his chest, arms, and neck in the world I knew him from. The longer Melody stayed in the tattoo parlour, the more I became curious as to what kind of tattoo she was having adorned on her young body. Perhaps she was having 'Fuck you, Momma' stencilled in red ink across her forehead? Perhaps she was having it adorned across her arse – so her Momma had something to read the next time she was giving Melody a good whipping? And that's what fascinated me about Melody. Unlike Isi-bore, the girl seemed to have some guts. She was something close to a rebel, even though she looked and dressed like a nun. I'd always wondered what really went on under a nun's habit. So with my curiosity getting the better of me, I swigged the last of the beer from the bottle and crossed the street to the tattooist.

Standing back from the window, I peered inside. Melody was lying face-down with her head turned away from the window. A thickset man, who himself had practically every inch of his body covered in tattoos, was bent over the girl as he inked hundreds of roses down the length of her back. The roses were bright pink.

I thought of what Noah had said, and now had no doubt that he'd been warning me not to hurt Melody Rose. Did Noah believe that I killed the girl? Then rubbing my temples, I turned away and headed back across the street to the bar. Did I kill the girl? Is that how she died? Why would I kill her? I wondered, taking a seat at the table by the window so I could keep an eye on the tattooist.

"Why did you kill me?" someone asked, and I looked up to see the bride was now waitressing my table. "Another beer?"

"Why don't you leave me alone?" I growled, leaping up from the table and sending it toppling over onto the floor.

I staggered back out onto the street, my brain aching. It felt like somebody was wringing it out like a wet cloth. Unable to bring myself to look back to see if the bride was following me, I headed back up the road and out of town. I reached the woods circling the lake, and collapsed against a tree. I waited for sundown and crept deeper into the woods. That was the night I finally put Mrs. Last out of her misery.

On the third day, Isi-bore stuck his head and shoulders out from below the grate. He looked pale and gaunt – like he had been ill in some way. I peered from behind a nearby tree and watched Isi-bore crawl out from beneath The Hollows. He closed the grate, hiding it from view with a handful of dead leaves and twigs. As I guessed he would, Isi-bore headed straight for the lake. The wind was blowing cold and hard, and his long coat flapped about his shins.

He has a coat at last! I noticed. Perhaps mummy reminded him to wear one, just in case he caught a cold.

I watched him race along the shore, then search the bush where he and Melody snuck away to work themselves into a frenzy over the gardening books Isi-bore stole from the local library. The boy came out of the bush and looked in both directions along the shore. I guessed Melody might be getting herself tattooed up, but I wasn't going to tell him that. I wouldn't even if I could. It wasn't my secret to tell. Pulling his coat tight about himself, Isidor headed back through the woods in the direction of Melody's home.

The boy lingered by the front gate. Then watching him draw a deep breath, he finally plucked up the guts to push it open and stroll up the front garden path. He knocked on the door while I hid amongst the trees. After what seemed like forever, the front door slowly swung open a fraction. I could just make out the lined and wrinkled face of Melody's mother peering out at Isi-bore. From my hiding place it was difficult for me to hear exactly what was being said. With the wind gusting in the tree branches above me, I could only get snippets of the conversation. I heard enough though to understand that Melody's mother was denying she even had a daughter. Was Melody dead already? Did that mean the photographer was on his or her way to the grate? But the photograph – it was of Melody and Isidor – I hadn't seen any picture taken of them. So did that mean the girl was still alive? My brain started to ache again and I pressed my fingertips against my temples. I wished now that I had asked more questions of Lilly Blu before I'd accepted this stupid fucking mission.

"You were too busy thinking about killing her," a voice said over my shoulder, and I didn't have to turn around to know it was the bride who was taunting me.

"How many ways have I got to tell you to fuck off," I snarled back at her. She must have finally got the message because she was gone already.

Needing to know if Melody were dead already, I sprang forward, taking on my wolf form. Just like I had in the woods, I slunk from my hiding place and around the side of the house.

"You do have a daughter, and her name is Melody..." I heard Isi-bore say.

"Yakadee – Yakadee – Yak!" the old bitch cackled. "I ain't listening because I never had no daughter! Now get off my porch!"

With my long, black tail arrowed out behind me, I jumped down over the wall and peered in through the basement window. I pushed it open with my long whiskered snout. As a wolf I was far too big to squeeze inside like I had before. I heard the front door slam shut from the other side of the house. I bounded back over the wall, and keeping flat like a lion creeping up on its prey, I made my way around the edge of the house. Peering around the wall, I watched Isidor, make his way back down the front garden path, then suddenly stop.

Did he know I was here?

He turned around, but instead of looking back in my direction, Isi-bore looked up at the house. A stupid-looking grin appeared on his face.

The fucking retard thinks this is funny, I thought.

Isi-bore then raised his hand and waved up at one of the bedroom windows. Then, without warning he took off his coat.

Another coat lost, I thought. Doesn't this kid feel the freaking cold?

Isi-bore stretched open his arms and revealed his wings. No sooner had they unfolded, his feet were lifting off the ground and he was floating upwards towards the window. I peered around the wall and looked upwards. Melody was at the window. She opened it.

They spoke, although from the ground I couldn't hear what it was they said. Isi-bore reached for her hand and pressed it flat against his chest.

Now that did surprise me. He wasn't even wearing a T-shirt. The boy was letting Melody touch his bare flesh. Perhaps things were looking up for these two. He then got even more daring as he leant through the open window, took Melody in his arms and swooped away with her in the direction of the lake.

How the fuck was I meant to follow the boy and girl if one of them could fly? I panted, setting off across the fields at great speed. With my long pink tongue lolling from between my jaws, I reached the treeline surrounding the lake. I sat on my giant haunches in the shadow of the trees and watched Isi-bore and

Melody standing together on the shore, by their secret camp. With fingers shaking, I watched Isi-bore reach out and slowly remove the girl's bonnet. Her long hair fell down her back. In the pink light of the fading sun sparkling off the lake, it made her hair shine like glitter.

Isi-bore gently sunk his hands into the thick curls of her hair. His wings rippled in the breeze, swooping down off the mountains in the distance.

"Do you like it?" Melody asked him, looking shy.

"It's beautiful," he told her.

Melody tenderly brushed her fingertips over his wings and down the length of his arms. "That's why you fled that day, wasn't it?" she said.

"Yes," he told her. "I could feel myself changing and I thought you would be scared of me."

Hearing this, I realised the true reason Isi-bore had fled that day on discovering Melody had been whipped by her mother. It wasn't because he lacked courage. He was going to change into his true Vampyrus self. He'd wanted to keep the fact that he was a monster hidden from Melody.

"You're not scared of me?" I heard him ask her, now that he had found the strength to truly be himself in front of her.

"How could I be scared of an angel?" Melody whispered, looking up into his eyes.

And again I wanted to be sick. I dropped down, placing my snout on my giant paws. But this time, I didn't feel sick because of their display of tenderness and love for each other – I felt sick because I envied them.

"Thank you," Isidor smiled down at her.

"Thank you for what?" Melody breathed.

"For liking me for who I am. For not laughing at me because I couldn't read and write," he told her.

"Thank you for not being cruel to me for how I dress and the way I live. Thank you for taking the loneliness away. I was so tired of being lonely, Isidor," Melody told him.

I couldn't stop the yelping sound that came from deep within me. I buried my snout beneath my paws and tried to block out the sound of my mother's voice that was now screaming in my ears.

"Paint! You can't paint! Even Father Paul was getting sick of you! He kept looking over at me and shaking his head in despair!"

I placed my paws over my ears to block out her voice. Father Paul had helped me to paint like Melody had helped Isidor to read. He hadn't laughed at me that night, nor had he looked at my mother with despair – just like Melody hadn't laughed at Isidor because he couldn't read or write. It was me who had laughed at Isidor. It was me who had called him a dumb-fuck. It was me. It was me.

You ruined Father Paul's evening and everybody else's. Now get to bed! My mother screeched inside of me.

I hadn't wanted to go to bed because I hadn't liked being on my own. I hated the loneliness I'd felt as a boy. I had learnt what true loneliness had been that Christmas my mother had left me alone in that café. I could still feel the emptiness at being left out of the fun they were having together. I understood Melody's loneliness. It was like a wide, black hole was sucking your soul out. Like Melody, I'd felt lonely. There is nothing worse than that feeling. Melody was so fucking lucky. Isidor and Melody were both so fucking lucky to have each other. And I couldn't help but feel myself hate them for that.

Chapter Twenty-Two

Potter

We sat in silence for most of the car journey back to Kiera's apartment. I was counting down the minutes until she finally said what I knew she had been dying to say since leaving the house of the dead boy.

"You heard what that woman said, didn't you?" Kiera finally remarked.

"What was that?" I said, lighting a cigarette and opening the window so I could blow the smoke out. The rain had stopped, but the wind battered into the side of her tiny car.

"The woman said that her brother claimed the teachers at the school were checking the girls to see if they had wings," Kiera said, watching the road ahead.

"The kid was freaking suicidal," I remarked. "He was delusional. He jumped in front of a train wearing his nephew's rubber Maggot Foreskin mask."

"Frogskin," Kiera corrected me.

"Whatever," I grunted. "The point I'm trying to make is that who knows what thoughts those wolves put inside those kids' heads."

"But what about the others?" she argued.

"What others?" I shot back.

"All those people in those newspaper clippings I've collected," Kiera reminded me.

"How many of those people went to schools like Ravenwood?" I tried to convince her. It wasn't easy to lie like this to Kiera. I had to keep reminding myself that this wasn't my Kiera. If she was eventually going to remember then so be it – but I couldn't be a part of that process. I shouldn't even be in the car with her right now. Both me and Jack had been warned not to get involved – not to change anything about the lives of the people we had come back to watch. I wondered how Jack was getting on. He had the easy mission. He only had to sit behind a tree and wait for the photographer to show up. How complex could that possibly get? He had no connections to either Melody or Isidor.

"What about those lumps on my back?" Kiera asked.

"Huh?" I said, pushing thoughts of Jack Seth from my mind.

"Those things sticking out of my back?" she sighed.

"I dunno," I shrugged. "Have you seen a doctor?"

"No," she said, shaking her head. "You're the only person who knows about them. I haven't even told my dad."

"How long have they been there?" I asked her.

"Just a couple of weeks," she explained. "They look like fingers."

"They look like tiny little lumps," I said, trying to play down her concerns. "They could be moles."

"Moles!" she scoffed. "The lumps feel hard, like bone."

"Okay so they're not moles, but that doesn't mean they're wings," I told her. "If I were you, I'd keep an eye on those lumps for the next couple of weeks, and if they're still there, go and get them checked out by your doctor."

"I guess you're right" she sighed, driving us through town towards her apartment.

I looked away, knowing that she would never know if I was right or wrong or what the lumps truly were. This Kiera didn't have a couple of weeks left to live. The next doctor to see Kiera would be pronouncing her life extinct.

Not wanting to think about that, I lit another cigarette and said, "Why did you think I'd been working with the wolves?"

"Sorry?" she frowned.

"When you found me hiding in the alleyway, you said that I was working with the wolves," I reminded her. "What did you mean by that?"

"You went to work with the wolves on that special investigations unit, remember?" she said, glancing at me.

"So?" I shrugged, knowing I was now talking about the Potter who had left Kiera in this *pushed* world and not me.

"That's why you said you were leaving, because you wanted to work with the wolves," Kiera said.

"Really? Did I say that?" I said, suspecting that the other Potter must be completely different from me, as I could never imagine myself volunteering to work alongside the wolves. Working against them, yes, but never with them.

"To be honest, you didn't say much, and that's why your leaving hurt so much," Kiera said. "I just woke up one morning and you had gone."

"I'm sorry," I whispered on behalf of the other Potter. Was he sorry? That I would never know.

"Why didn't you call me?" she asked, sounding hurt rather than pissed off.

"I thought…" I started.

"I tried calling you but your phone was always switched off," she said. "I called 'C' Division and they said you were away on special operations and un-contactable."

"I'm sorry…" I tried again. Why was I apologising for this other Potter? It should be him, not me. Sure I'd screwed up plenty in the past, but for once this wasn't one of my fuck-ups!

"So you keep saying, but you haven't explained why you're back," she said.

"Let's just say things didn't work out for me with the wolves," I said. "They never really have."

Before Kiera had a chance to question me any further of the disappearance of the other Potter, the sound of Bruno Mars singing *Just the way you are* came from her coat pocket. Taking one hand from the wheel, Kiera pulled out the phone and passed it to me.

"Answer that," she said. "I can't talk now, I'm driving."

Turning the phone over in my hands, I couldn't help but notice the crescent-shaped moon logo on the back. I hit the answer button and pressed the phone to my ear.

"Hello," I said.

"Sorry, I must have the wrong number," the voice said.

"Who do you want to speak to?" I asked.

"Kiera… Kiera Hudson," the voice came back.

"This is Kiera's phone," I told him.

"Who is this?" he asked, sounding confused.

"Potter," I said.

"Potter? But I thought you were..." the voice trailed off into silence.

"Were what?" I cut in, as Kiera steered the car towards the kerb and killed the engine.

"I thought you had left," and this time his voice sounded shocked rather than confused.

"Who is this?" I asked.

"John, John Miles. You remember me, don't you, Potter?" the voice said.

"How could I ever forget you, *Sparky*," I scowled, handing Kiera back the phone.

"Hey, John," Kiera said.

She listened while he spoke and I watched her.

"And the intel is good this time around?" she asked him. "It's definitely going to be tonight?"

She listened again.

"Okay," she said. "I'll see you at ten tonight."

Kiera finished the call and placed the phone back into her pocket.

"What are you staring at?" she asked, looking back at me.

"So what's happening tonight at ten?" I asked, trying to sound casual.

"Why? Are you jealous?" she smiled.

"What, of Sparky?" I scoffed. "Yeah, I'd love a face full of zits and a broken pair of glasses. I'm jealous, all right."

Kiera started up the car again and steered away from the kerb. "If you must know, we've had some information that there is going to be a robbery tonight. We've had a spate of robberies in the area over the last few months, and we haven't been able to catch the gang yet."

My heart leapt in my chest and I looked at Kiera. "Robbery, did you say?" knowing that Kiera died in a shootout while attending a robbery.

"Hopefully we'll catch them tonight," she said.

141

"Who's we?" I asked, fearing that tonight was going to be the night Kiera died in this *pushed* world.

"John and me," Kiera explained.

With my eyes popping in my head, I stared at her and said, "Kiera you can't stake out the scene of a robbery with just Sparky. You're gonna need backup."

"Like I said, John and I are the only cops left in this town who actually care about solving real crime. The wolves aren't interested," Kiera explained.

"But you might get hurt," I told her – I tried to warn her.

Pulling the car up outside her apartment block, she turned off the engine and looked at me. "Then come with us. You're still a cop. It would be like the old times, Potter." She smiled.

Please don't smile at me, I thought and looked away. However much I wanted to go with Kiera and be her backup, I couldn't. I wasn't to change anything here. And if I didn't change what I feared was going to happen tonight, then I couldn't bear to watch Kiera get shot dead. She might not be my Kiera – but to watch her die would be unbearable.

"I can't come tonight," I breathed, pushing open the car door and climbing out.

"Why not?" she asked, frowning at me over the roof of the car. "Got a better offer?"

"No, I don't have a better offer..." I started.

"Then what's the problem?" she said, fishing her front door keys from her pocket and heading towards the apartment block. "It would be great to have you there. I know John would like to see you again."

If he was anything like the Sparkly that I knew before the world got *pushed*, he wouldn't be glad to see me at all. I didn't tell Kiera this, and instead, I said, "I can't come with you tonight, however much I want to."

"Why not?" she said, standing in the open doorway of the apartment block and looking back at me. She had a confused look in her eyes. "I thought you'd come back, Potter?"

"I should've never come back," I said, wanting to go with

Kiera on the stakeout but knowing that I couldn't. "It was a mistake."

Looking at me with tears suddenly standing in her eyes, Kiera said, "Go on, Potter, run away again. After all, that's what you do best." She stepped into the hallway, and without looking back, she slammed the front door in my face.

"Kiera," I whispered. "I'm sorry."

Chapter Twenty-Three

Jack

I had to sit and endure listening to Isi-bore read Melody a story he had written. I lay silently a few feet away from the bush where Melody sat and listened to Isi-bore read his story. At first I thought it was going to be a bunch of bullshit and some half-witted ideas strung together. But as Isi-bore continued to read, my ears pricked up. He spoke of a boy who was saved from his unhappy life by Marilyn Monroe who stepped out of a picture and pushed him into a different *where* and *when*. I thought of Lilly Blu and how much she looked like Marilyn Monroe, and how she had sent us to a different *where* and *when*. Had Isi-bore really written a story about himself and Lilly Blu, or was it simply a coincidence?

My head hurt again, and I rolled over in the fallen leaves that covered the floor of the wood. Was I looking for stuff – connections – that weren't really there? I needed to get back to my own *where* and *when* and put this shit behind me. With my head feeling like it was going to split open at any moment, I climbed onto all fours and was about to head back towards the grate, when I heard Melody say something that made me stop in my tracks and look back over my shoulder at the secret camp.

"The ending was magical," she said. "Just imagine if you could go someplace else – to a place where you could be happy. That would be magical, right?"

"I guess," Isi-bore said.

"You know it would be magical or you wouldn't have written that story," Melody said. "That story was about me, wasn't it?

It could be about any of us, I thought, my tail wagging to and fro in the wind.

"You had a magical place you used to go to", the bride said, suddenly appearing beside me. She gently stroked my coat with one of her lace-gloved hands. "Your magical place used to be Father Paul's house. That was your sanctuary, wasn't it, poor old Jack?"

"Yes," I said, slowly nodding my head, remembering how free I felt there – away from the cruelty shown to me at home.

I looked away from the bride and in the direction of Melody's voice as I heard her say to Isi-bore, "The only difference is that I don't have anyone to take me someplace else, some place magical."

To hear her say this, made my heart suddenly ache, for I knew that Melody Rose wasn't heading anywhere magical. She was going to be dead soon and there wasn't anything I could do to stop that. That wasn't the reason I'd been sent back.

"And why should I give a shit anyway?" I said, turning towards the bride, but she had gone again.

Looking back at the bush where Melody and Is-bore hid, I told myself the girl meant nothing to me. Her life was her problem. I had enough problems of my own. There was a rustling sound behind me, and half expecting to see that fucking bride stalking me again, I looked back to see three youths creeping through the woods towards the shore. I could see two teenage boys and a girl. One of the boys had the biggest buckteeth I'd ever seen. They hung over his bottom lip, giving him the appearance of a donkey.

I watched them step from out of the woods and onto the shore. Isi-bore and Melody must have heard them, as they suddenly appeared from inside.

"For God's sake," I heard Isi-bore groan out loud at the sight of the others.

"You got me in the shit good and proper the other day with that cop!" the boy, who looked like Rabbit from the Winnie Pooh books, scowled. "It was you who stole that book, and you weren't even man enough to own up to it."

"You shouldn't have stolen my coat," Isi-bore shot back.

So this was the thief who stole Isi-bore's coat, I thought, deciding not to head back to the grate just yet. This could be interesting.

The thief then noticed Melody standing behind Isi-bore and said, "Whoa! Who have we got here?"

"They've been getting it on in the bushes!" the fucking ugly kid sniggered with excitement.

"With her?" the teenage girl said in disbelief. "But she's, like, some kinda nun or something."

"It's the quiet ones you have to watch," the thief said, reaching forward. He tried to lift up the hem of Melody's dress.

I shot to my haunches, eyes flashing bright and yellow. Melody slapped his hand away.

"I just want to see your titties," the thief smirked.

"Fuck off!" Melody hissed.

Good girl, I thought, then looked through the bushes at Isi-bore. What the fuck was he waiting for? The guy was messing with his girl.

"Woo-hoo!" the ugly-fucker laughed, clapping his hands feverishly together. "The nun swears!"

Now if I had to step in here, he was the first fucker to get his throat torn out. I wonder if he would find that so fucking funny.

But I couldn't get involved. What if it was these kids that killed Melody? Did I have to sit back and watch? I would have to. I couldn't get involved here. And why would I want to? Then to my surprise, Isi-bore positioned himself in front of Melody.

"Why don't you three just go away?" he said.

Why don't you three go away? I mimicked inside my head. What the fuck was that all about? If I hadn't have seen Isi-bore's wings with my own eyes, I would have never believed he was a Vampyrus. This kid must be an embarrassment to their race.

"Why should you get all the fun?" the thief glared at Isi-bore. "How about the nun gives me and my friend Barry over here a hand job each and we won't tell her mum what she's been up to in the bushes with you."

"That's not going to happen," Isi-bore said.

Who does Isi-bore think he is? Clark-fucking-Kent? Rip his fucking face off! I felt like howling at him. The thief just said he wants your girl to give him a hand job!

"What? She's not going to give us a hand job, or we're not going to tell her mum that she's been screwing you?" the thief said, taking a step closer to Isi-bore.

"Neither is gonna happen," Isi-bore told him, still standing in front of Melody.

"And you're gonna stop me, I guess?" the thief said, raising his fists.

Do something, Isi-bore, or you're gonna get your face smashed in. Why wouldn't he fight?

Instead he said, "What are you gonna do, Ray, whoop my arse? Beat me? *Shoot* me with one of your dad's big fuck-off guns? Then what are ya gonna do? Get Melody to whack you off? Then what? Beat her, too?"

Don't give the thief ideas, you dumb prick! I felt like howling.

I watched the thief take another step towards Isi-bore and roll up his sleeves, readying himself to beat seven kinds of shit out of him. This was gonna be ugly. I didn't know if I could watch.

"C'mon, Isidor, let's just get outer here," Melody pleaded, pulling at Isi-bore's sleeve.

This was just embarrassing to watch. Just when I thought I was going to witness Isi-bore get a good kick in, he glanced at Melody and said, "What, and spend the rest of our lives running from *bullies* like him?"

"You should listen to your girlfriend and run while you still can," the thief threatened. I hated to agree with him, but yeah – Isi-bore should make a run for it.

But to my surprise, Isi-bore didn't run away, he stayed and stood his ground.

"Do what you have to do then," he said, standing tall. "Beat me, kill me! But I promise you, even if I have to crawl on my hands and fucking knees, I'm gonna tell every last motherfucker in this town that really, you're just a scared little boy."

I shook my head in disbelief. Did Isi-bore just say the fuck word? It wasn't only me who was stunned by this. The thief and his friends looked at each other, mouths open like drowning fish.

"Would daddy be proud of his son if he knew that he bullied girls, tried to get them to whack him off?" Isi-bore continued. He was on a roll. "I reckon he'll be bursting with so much pride, he'll award you the 'Jerk-off of the year award'!"

At the mention of the thief's father, the boy flinched backwards as if Isi-bore had punched him somehow. A strange look came over Isi-bore's face – like he'd just figured something out – seen some important clue he had been missing. Now perhaps he was going to rip the thief's head off?

But instead of turning violent, Isi-bore said with a knowing smile, "I get it, I get it! So who's scared of their daddy then?"

"Shut your fucking mouth!" the thief groaned. Again I couldn't help but notice that the boy looked like he had been punched by Isi-bore. It was like Isi-bore was beating the thief but without having to use violence.

"So daddy doesn't love you? Is that it?" Isi-bore said.

"*Shut-up!*" the thief cried out as if in pain.

"Or is it that daddy loves you *too* much? The bad kinda love that he says is perfectly okay, but just don't tell your momma about it!" It was like Isi-bore had the bigger kid against the ropes but hadn't thrown a single punch.

"*Shut-up! Shut-up! Shut-up!*" the boy wailed, placing his hands over his ears.

"I'll shut-up if you promise you'll leave Melody alone, and that goes for your friends," Isi-bore said. He was now in charge and he knew it. His voice was different – stronger and firmer – but not angry and full of hate.

"I promise," the thief whispered.

"I can't hear you!" Isi-bore said.

"*I promise!*" the boy cried.

"I think at last we've come to an understanding, and we got there without the use of any violence. A first for you, I suspect," Isi-bore said, staring at the boy. "Now get out of here!"

The thief turned and fled up the shore with his friends following him. I waited for them to disappear from view, then peered through the bushes at Isi-bore and wondered if he was the dumb-arse I'd first believed him to be. He had truly beaten the thief who had stolen his coat, without killing him or having *fun* with his family.

I watched Isi-bore release his wings from beneath his arms.

He swooped up into the sky, holding Melody in his arms.

Way to go, Isidor, I thought.

Chapter Twenty-Four

Potter

I wandered around with my thumb up my arse for the rest of the day. There was little point hiding out in the alleyway, Kiera would only see me. If the photographer was going to come, it would be after Kiera was killed tonight. I knew Kiera would be leaving her apartment to join Sparky on the stakeout sometime after ten. I would come back then.

However hard I tried to *push* thoughts of Kiera's death from my mind, I couldn't. I mooched about the desolate town of Havensfield, collar turned up against the rain and the cold. I was so lost to my thoughts that I took no notice of those who passed me by on the streets. I struggled with the fact that I had walked away from her again. Again? I hadn't run out on her. That had been the other Potter. It should be that Potter who was wandering around the tiny cobbled streets of Havensfield, feeling guilty and ashamed. Why should I carry his burden? I hadn't done anything wrong – not this time around at least. Perhaps if he only knew what was going to happen tonight, then he might come and save her. I was told not to change anything here, but if he saved her, then technically it wouldn't be me who stopped her from being killed. Did that stack up? Did it work? But if I somehow let him know, it would still be me who put in motion a chain of events which would change what happened to Kiera. But if I told him, he could do what he wanted with that information. That would be down to him and not me.

But where was this Potter? Where would I find him in this world?

"Lilly told you that you couldn't come in contact with your own self in this world," a voice said from behind me.

I spun around in the wind and rain to find the little girl sitting on a wooden bench next to a red public phone box.

"What did you say?" I asked, rubbing rain from my face with my hand.

"You can't see yourself in this place, Potter," the little girl smiled at me. She seemed immune to the fact that the rain ran through her hair and soaked her bright red dress. She was short enough for her feet not to touch the pavement, and she swung them slowly back and forth like pendulums in a grandfather clock.

"Who are you?" I asked, sitting next to her on the bench. "Do I know you?"

"I know you," she smiled. Then jumping from the bench, both her feet splashing into a puddle, she waved and said, "See you later..."

"Alligator," I whispered as she blew away to nothing on a gust of wind. I continued to sit on the bench in the wind and rain. Cars crawled slowly by, the sound of the cars tyres hissing on the wet tarmac. Soaked through with the rain and feeling cold, I got up, yanked open the door of the phone box, and stepped inside. It would offer me some protection until the rain stopped. The phone box smelt of stale urine. Even in a sleepy little town like Havensfield, there were obviously people who still felt the urge to take a piss in the phone box. Fucking animals, I thought, then looked at the phone. I had an idea. Lilly had said that seeing my other self would be really bad – whatever the fuck that meant. How bad was bad? Were we talking about opening or closing a few more of those cracks? How bad could that be? Noah was opening cracks like they were going out of fashion. Or did Lilly mean completely screwing up the whole space-time continuum thing? What did she know anyhow – it wasn't like she was Doc Brown or anything. They had the same colour hair and style, but that was about it.

I looked at the phone. Speaking to the other Potter wouldn't be like seeing him – would it? I picked up the receiver. I searched my pockets with me free hand. I had no money. I wanted to speak to a cop after all, so why shouldn't I dial 999? I knew the number was for emergencies – but this was one. A woman was going to get killed tonight.

I dialled three nines and the phone was answered almost immediately.

151

"What is your emergency?" the operator asked. Her voice sounded nasally and far off.

Where did I start? "I'd like to speak to a cop..."

"So you want the police?" the woman asked.

"Not all of them, just one would do, his name is..." I started.

"This line is for emergency calls only..." she cut in.

"And this is an emergency..." I tried again.

"What is your emergency?" she asked again.

This was getting to be fucking pointless. We were just going around in circles. "Look, lady, I desperately need to get hold of a police officer named Potter. Sean Potter. I wouldn't be calling this number if it wasn't real important. Please help me."

There was a silence at the other end of the line, and I half expected the line to go dead. The woman suddenly spoke again. "Where is Officer Potter based?"

"All I know is that he works out of 'C' Division in the county of Havenshire," I said, grateful that she was helping me.

"One moment, caller, I'll put you through, but please remember that this line is for emergency calls only," she reminded me.

"I'm sorry," I said.

I could hear several clicking sounds on the line then a ringing tone. The phone was answered at the other end.

"C – Division – special ops department, how can I help you?" A male and sullen-sounding voice came down the line.

"Can I speak to Police Constable Potter please?" I said.

There was a long pause.

"And you are?" the voice eventually asked.

I'm him, I felt like saying, but instead I said, "I'm his brother."

"Brother?" the voice came back. Was that a note of suspicion I could detect – or was I being paranoid?

"What is your name?" the man asked.

"Funnily enough it's Potter, but then again it would be seeing as we're brothers," I sighed impenitently.

Another long silence, the only sound was the rain lashing against the telephone box.

"When was the last time you saw your brother?" the male asked.

"Not for a long time," I said, sensing that something wasn't quite right.

"And your family?" he said.

"What has my family got to do with this?" I breathed. "I haven't seen them in years either." This wasn't a lie. "We're not very close."

"That would explain it then..." he started.

"Explain what?" I cut in.

"Why you haven't heard the news."

"What news?" he was starting to piss me off.

Another long silence.

I heard the guy on the other end of the line draw in a deep breath then say, "I'm sorry to inform you, Mr. Potter, but your brother is dead."

Now it was my turn to be silent. I was dead. The other me was dead in this world. "How?" I stammered. "How did I... how did my brother die?"

"He was murdered," the man said, still sounding sullen.

"By who?" I shot back.

"That we don't know..." he said.

"What do you mean, you don't know?" I asked, feeling confused.

"The investigation is still on-going..."

"Who is the investigating officer?" I snapped. "I want to speak to them."

"I'm afraid that's not possible," the voice said. "The investigating officer is out of the office at the moment."

"Give me their name and I'll call back," I said.

"Detective John Miles," the man said. "Do you want his number?"

"I've already got that officer's number," I said, placing the receiver back into its cradle. "No wonder Sparky sounded so fucking shocked when I answered Kiera's phone. He thinks I'm dead."

I pushed open the phone box and stepped back out into the rain. It was getting dark now, as the night drew in and Kiera's death got closer. I wandered up the street in the direction of Kiera's apartment. What did I do? I knew what I should do and that was to forget about what I had learnt, go back to the alleyway, wait for the photographer to show up, unmask him, then head back to Lilly Blu at the station and to my Kiera. But I couldn't forget. Sparky believed me to be dead. He was investigating my murder. He had sounded surprised when he spoke to me, but not surprised enough. As far as he was concerned, he was speaking to a freaking ghost.

I thought you had left, he had said down the phone to me. Shouldn't that have been, *I thought you were dead...*?

There was something seriously fucking wrong here, and just like in the world before it got *pushed*, Sparky was at the centre of it. The wolf was fucking with me and probably with the Kiera of this world, too. It was Sparky who had invited her to the place where she would lose her life. That was more than just a coincidence. Unbeknown to Kiera, Sparky was pushing her towards her inevitable death and I was gonna *push* right back.

Chapter Twenty-Five

Jack

The next time I saw Isidor, he was crawling once again from beneath The Hollows. And just like he had before, he made his way alone through the woods and towards the town of Lake Lure. At first I thought perhaps he was heading for Melody's home again. But he did a detour to the local swimming pool. The car park in front of the building was full of school buses and parked cars. Flags had been hung around the eaves of the building like there was some kind of celebration about to take place. From a small grassy knoll, I stood back and watched as Isi-bore blended in with the humans filing into the building. Liking his idea, I came down from my vantage point, joined the end of the line, and went into the pool with the others.

A woman in front of me turned, and with a look of excitement on her face, she said, "What swimming team is your child in?"

"How should I know, lady?" I shrugged.

"You do have a child at this school, don't you?" she said with a look of growing concern.

"Of course I do," fixing her with a stare so she could look into my eyes and see the fun we could have together.

With her cheeks blushing, she tried to break my stare but couldn't. "So how come you don't know what swimming team your child is in?" she said, her voice wavering, as she continued to look into my blazing eyes.

"Haven't seen the kid since it was just a baby," I told her. "Only just got out of jail."

"Out of jail," she gasped. I couldn't figure out if she was shocked by what she saw me doing to her in my eyes, or the fact that I'd just gotten out of jail.

"What were you in jail for?" she almost panted.

"I killed twelve women," I grinned down into her eyes.

"Really?" she gasped, putting a hand to her throat.

"No, I'm just kidding," I smiled, leaning in close to her. "I killed sixty-three. How about we even up the number and make it sixty-four." I then snaked my hand around her waist and squeezed her arse.

"What are you doing?" she breathed, still looking into my eyes.

"Just having fun with your buns," I whispered into her ear. I felt her shudder against me.

"Hey what's going on?" I heard a bewildered and concerned voice say.

I looked over the lady's shoulder to see a dumpy-looking bald man.

"Say what?" I said, looking at him.

"That's my wife's arse you're grabbing," he scowled, his heavy jowls wobbling.

Now that I was no longer looking into the woman's eyes, she stepped back from me, then turned to look at her husband.

"What's going on, Jill?" the man asked, holding two dripping ice-cream cones in his podgy hands.

"Huh?" she said, running a hand through her hair and looking as if she had no idea what had just happened. She probably didn't, in all fairness.

"I went to get some ice-cream, only to come back to find you in this man's arms," he said, looking more upset than angry. "You promised me nothing like this would ever happen again after I caught you with Bill."

Jill and Bill, I smiled inside. You couldn't make it up. I looked the woman up and down and how I envied good old Bill, whoever he was.

The woman glanced up at me, then back at her husband. As if now remembering what she had seen in my eyes, she grabbed her husband by the arm and said, "C'mon, let's go and find some seats."

"Who was that man?" I heard her husband demand as they walked away.

"I don't know... it was nothing..." I heard the woman start to say.

Knowing that I would have to look the woman up before I returned to my own *where* and *when*, I took my seat amongst the other parents gathered around the edge of the pool. I sat low in my seat and watched the show. There was a raised platform on which a row of adults were gathered on. I guessed the people sitting on the seats were the school teachers. I noticed a vacant seat and wondered if that had been where Mrs. Last was meant to have sat.

Oops! I thought. Ah well, never mind, she's probably a lot more comfortable lying down in the woods. I wiggled in my seat. The chairs weren't very comfortable anyway. I'd probably done her a favour in a strange way.

The headmaster stood and welcomed the parents and the mayor of the town. He explained that it was the twenty-fifth anniversary of the school and a swimming gala had been arranged to show off the proud sportsmanship of the school and to celebrate the opening of the school all those years ago. As the headmaster stood and talked bollocks, I looked around the swimming pool. In the back row sat Isi-bore. Once the headmaster had finished boring us all near to unconsciousness, the swimming gala began. I didn't know what was worse, listening to the headmaster, or watching the school kids swimming back and forth in the water. I glanced back at Isi-bore, and by the soppy look on his face I could tell he was enjoying it. Why wasn't I surprised by that?

Just when I thought I couldn't bear it any longer, the headmaster stood up again and addressed the crowd.

"I'm sure you'll all agree that this has been a wonderful event today."

Really?

"It goes to illustrate the school's team spirit and love of sports. But, ladies and gentlemen, the day is not over yet," he continued. "We now have something very special for you. We are very proud of this young athlete. I understand she has been working tirelessly for some weeks to put on a spectacular finale. It is with great pleasure that I now introduce, Melody Rose."

Okay, so this is why Isi-bore is really here. He wanted to catch a glimpse of his girl in her swimsuit.

Pervert!

I was definitely warming to him.

Melody came out of the dressing room and walked silently along the edge of the pool. With her head bowed, she made her way to the diving board. She was dressed in a long, white dressing gown, which trailed out behind her. She kind of reminded me of my stalker – the bride. I pushed thoughts of her from my head. Melody's hair was tucked out of sight beneath a swimming cap. She slowly climbed the ladder to the highest board. Everyone in the crowd sat with their tilted heads on their necks as they watched her progress. She glanced only once at Isi-bore. I looked back at him. What was going on between these two? Did they have something planned? But by the look of bewilderment on his face, I sensed that he didn't know what was about to happen either. The audience sat in a hushed silence.

Melody reached the highest diving board. She stood motionless, like a statue. Then suddenly, she peeled back the dressing gown and let it slide away. The crowd gasped, and I smiled. The rose tattoos I had seen on her back now covered every inch of her naked body. All of the roses were closed, apart from one covering her right breast – just over her heart. This rose was open and full of colour. Melody stood, back straight and removed the swimming cap. Her once blond hair now flowed thick and bright pink down her back. I looked over my shoulder at Isi-bore and he was grinning from ear to ear. He didn't look like he was getting his rocks off because the girl he loved was standing naked before him – he was grinning with pride.

I looked back at her and continued to smile, too. I had never spoken to the girl – she didn't know that I existed, but that didn't stop me feeling strangely proud of her, too. I was proud of her because she might as well of had *Fuck-Off* tattooed across her forehead in red ink. She was telling everyone in this room – everyone that she might ever come across – that she was Melody

Rose and she was different. She was telling them all she wasn't ashamed to be different and she no longer cared what they or anyone else thought of her.

Good for you, Melody Rose, I smiled inside. *Good for you!*

Then, looking out across the pool at her friend Isidor, she said, "For one day, Isidor, I just want to be me."

She then dropped over the edge of the diving board. With a lump growing in my throat, I watched her splash into the water below. The crowd lost sight of her and the stunned silence was deafening. Then she appeared from beneath the water with the biggest of smiles on her face. And for the first time I realised she truly did look beautiful. Something then happened that I wasn't expecting. The other pupils gathered around the pool jumped from their seats and started to cheer. The noise was ear-splitting. Hearing their cheers, Melody started to punch the air with her fist. It was like she was starting a revolution, not only in the room, but inside the other kids gathered beside the pool. It was like an electric charge had been set off. I looked at all the smiling and beaming faces of the school children, and knew that Melody's defiance meant something to them too. Not one of them would ever forget this. They would tell their husbands and wives, recount this story to their children, their grandchildren, each of them never forgetting the importance of being true to yourself. Not to ever let anyone change you.

"Doesn't that mean you, too, Jack?" a voice said, over the roar of the crowd.

I looked sideways, to find the bride now sitting next to me.

"It doesn't apply to me," I said.

"You let your mother change you," she said. "You didn't have to turn out like her. Melody refuses to be like her mother. Melody's life has been very much like yours..."

"There's one difference between Melody and me," I said, getting up from my seat, not wanting to hear any more.

"And what's that?" the bride called after me.

"Melody is stronger than me... she is better than me," I said, walking away through the roaring crowds.

I looked back only once, to see Melody being dragged from the pool by one of her teachers. I just hoped she was strong enough to deal with the hurt that she would inevitably receive for making a stand. And perhaps that's why I never made a stand – because I was sick of all the hurt. It seemed easier to hurt than let yourself be hurt. Both Isidor and Melody had confronted their demons without becoming a monster like I had.

Chapter Twenty-Six

Potter

I stood in the mouth of the alleyway and looked out at Kiera's apartment. It was fully dark now. The rain had stopped at last. The air was still damp, but there were very little clouds in the sky, and the stars shone through, as did the moon. I still wasn't certain of what I was going to do, but I had to do something. Lilly's warning kept circling around and around in my mind. With the other Potter dead, who was left to warn Kiera of the trap I feared Sparky had set for her tonight?

"But you're not meant to be saving her, Potter," a voice from beside me said.

I looked down to see the young girl standing behind me in the alleyway. Her pale white face looked up at me from the dark like a small moon.

"Hey, little girl," I said.

"Yes?" she smiled.

"Scram!" I barked.

Just like she had before, she waved her corpse-white hand at me, then melted away, back into the darkness she had crept from.

I looked back at the apartment block across the street. The light in Kiera's living room was turned off, sending her apartment into darkness. My heart started to race. The front door swung open and Kiera appeared from the other side of it. Her long, jet-black hair hung straight on either side of her pale face. Her lips were full red, and her eyes bright. She was dressed all in black, as was standard on these types of operations. There was no difference between this Kiera and the Kiera I had fallen in love with. Were they not both the same? I wondered as she approached her car. My heart started to quicken. Wasn't this Kiera really my Kiera, separated only by a piece of tracing paper? Whether she was mine or not, I couldn't let Kiera walk into a trap. I couldn't let her die, however bad the consequences might be for me. Maybe Jack should have come? I wondered as Kiera opened the car door and climbed inside. Maybe he would have been able to keep his head better than me. I doubted it – but perhaps.

I heard the sound of the car engine rumble into life. Kiera switched on the headlights, then pulled away in the car just as I pounced across the street.

"Potter!" Kiera screamed, slamming on the brakes.

I pressed the palms of my hands flat against the car bonnet.

"Have you lost your mind?" she said, winding down the window and looking at me in shock. "I could've killed you."

"I changed my mind about tonight," I said, coming around the side of the car and opening the passenger door. "I'm coming with you." I sat down, drawing my knees up until they almost touched my chin.

"Why the change of heart?" she said, looking sideways at me in the dark, the engine ticking over.

"That's the problem," I said, looking back at her. "My heart has never changed from the way I feel about you, and it never will."

As soon as the words had passed over my lips, I wished I could've taken them back. I'd just wanted to be kind, but I had instead said the cruellest thing. If Kiera did survive tonight then she would think I was back in her life. But the Potter in this world was dead and I had to go back to mine.

Kiera looked at me and I prepared myself for another punch in the face. With tears standing in the corner of her eyes, she leant forward and kissed me softly on the cheek.

"What was that for?" I asked her.

"For being the most infuriating man I have ever met," she whispered, turning front and setting off down the road.

"Is that a good thing?" I asked.

"Not for me, I guess," she half-smiled to herself.

I wasn't sure if she was paying me a compliment or not, so I didn't say anything and lit another cigarette. If Kiera survived tonight, then before I left, I would tell her the truth. Kiera deserved that. I would tell her everything. I would show her my wings and tell her to go run and hide and to never look back. If that fucked things up in some way, then I would have to live with it. What was Lilly going to do – send me to my room? And besides, what would she do if she was in my situation and she had the chance of saving her daughters – saving Murphy?

"But she isn't your Kiera Hudson," a voice whispered.

I looked over my shoulder, half expecting to see that little girl waving at me from the backseat. But she wasn't there. It had been my own voice warning me this time around.

"Is everything okay?" Kiera asked. "You look kinda stressed."

"It's nothing," I lied, looking front again. "It's been a while since I've been on a stakeout."

"It will be fun," she smiled at me. "Just like the old days. We met on an undercover job, remember?"

"How could I ever forget?" I smiled back.

"Can you remember what you called me?" she asked.

How the fuck should I know? I wanted to get off this topic, and fast. "Mmm... I can't really remember."

"You were a real jerk," she said.

"That doesn't sound like me," I smiled at her.

"You called me Miss Marple, and can you remember why?" she glanced at me.

"Because... because..." I said, acting as if the memory was just out of reach.

"Because the dead body of that kid was hidden in the boot of the father's car just like I said it would be, and you said it would be hidden in the attic," she said, filling in the blanks for me.

"Oh yeah," I said. "How could I ever forget that?"

"You know what my sense of smell can be like," she said. "That's another reason I knew that you were spying on me from that alleyway."

I thought Kiera saw things – not smelt things. So there were subtle differences between the two Kieras. "You could smell the cigarette smoke?"

"Sweat! That's what I could smell, Potter," she laughed. "You hadn't showered in days. You stank!"

"Thanks," I muttered, looking out of the window and into the dark. Not wanting to discuss my personal hygiene – or lack of it – I said, "Do you think Sparky will be surprised to see me again?"

"I guess, you've been away for more than a year," she said. "He won't be as surprised as I was when I found you sitting in my apartment."

"I wouldn't count on it," I muttered, flicking the cigarette end through the gap in the window. "So where are we meeting up with Sparky?"

"Just on the outskirts of town," she said, driving the car through the night.

"Out of town?" I frowned. "What's there to rob in the middle of nowhere? If a place was going to be hit, then wouldn't it be a bank, or..."

"It's Bleak Point Railway Station," she said.

"A railway station?" I asked. Now why wasn't I surprised about that? It kinda made sense in a perverted kind of way.

"I know, you would never have guessed it," she said. "That's why this team of robbers have been so freaking hard to catch. They're not committing their crimes in town, but out of town in the remotest of places. Churches, farmhouses, and now a remote railway station."

"What are they gonna find to steal at a railway station? A bunch of goddamn tickets?" I said.

"The ATM," she said. "It will be full of cash."

"Will it?" I said, not convinced. "If I were gonna go to all the trouble of ripping out an ATM, I would do it at a gas station."

"You would," she laughed softly.

"Think about it for a minute," I said. "Hit a gas station in town and you could be on a motorway and miles away from the scene of the crime in minutes. Hit a place in the middle of fucking nowhere, and you could spend the next six hours or so driving around with your thumb up your arse because you've got lost – especially in the dark. It's pitch black out here."

"I guess that's what they like about it," she said, peering into the darkness ahead of us. Then, slowly she steered her car down a narrow overgrown dirt track. Wild undergrowth scratched the

164

sides of her car. Ahead, I saw the red reflectors of a car shining back in Kiera's headlights. "There's John," she whispered, bringing the car to a stop.

The driver's door swung open ahead of us down the track. Both me and Kiera got out and walked towards the tall figure that loomed ahead of us in the darkness. I approached the man who was investigating my murder. I glanced at Kiera, then ahead again.

Sparky stepped out of the darkness. His face was nothing more than a red rash of spots. His glasses sat lopsided across the bridge of his nose, one arm held together with a sticking plaster. His black greasy hair was smeared to one side across his brow.

"This is a surprise," he said, offering me his hand to shake.

I lit a cigarette, and peering through the smoke at him, I smiled and said, "You look like you've seen a ghost, Sparky."

Chapter Twenty-Seven

Jack

I'd gone back to the grate and waited for either Isi-bore, Melody, or perhaps even the photographer to show up. I no longer really cared which. I'd had enough of this world and wanted to go back. But what did I have to go back to? My brother had gone – sacrificed himself for our sister – a sister who would never want anything to do with me. And could I blame her? No – not at all. I had held her captive and forced her to watch me torture her father to death, for fuck's sake. How did anyone ever begin to forgive something like that? All they would ever want is revenge. But Kiera had had her chance for revenge. She could've given me over to Murphy and Potter. Kiera hadn't, though. Kiera had let me go. I had wanted her to make her choice and as I sat in the wood and stared at the grate, I knew in my twisted little heart what that choice had really been about. I had wanted her to choose me. I had been so desperate for Kiera – my sister – to choose me over her own father, her lover Potter, and her friends. No one had ever chosen me. Even the man I had loved as a father had chosen Kiera over me. Fuck, that hurt and I wanted her to hurt, too. If she felt the hurt I had, then perhaps she would become a monster too – just like I had. But she hadn't become a monster, even after everything I had put her through. Why hadn't she given in to the curse like I had? She was half wolf too. What was so different about Kiera and me?

"She chose differently to you, Jack," the voice said.

Without even looking up, I knew the bride was close again. I didn't want to see her standing there all in white, that veil flapping about her face.

"Go away," I whispered, my head hung low.

"Poor little Jack," the bride said with a sneer. "Poor little boy who got left behind by his mummy. Poor little Isi-bore who can't read and write and was given up by his mummy. Poor little Melody Doze who was whipped by her momma and will be killed by her. Poor little Kiera Hudson who was deceived by her mother and betrayed by you and her friends. You're all the same, but with one difference, Jack."

"Shut the fuck up!" I seethed, prodding at my temples with my fingertips again.

The bride continued, despite my protests. "Every one of you had a choice to make. You could let your past with all its pain defeat you or make you. Kiera and the others got back up every time they were knocked down. But you chose not to get back up, Jack. *That's* the difference between Kiera and you. Kiera is a fighter and you're a killer. There is a big difference, Jack."

Snarling, I lept from the base of the tree. I grabbed hold of the bride's throat with my claws. I ripped back the veil, wanting to look upon her face, but there was nothing there. My claws were clutching at air. I dropped to my knees and howled. Why was I being haunted like this? But I now understood I had been haunted by nothing more than my own guilt and shame.

With my claws covering my emaciated face, I howled in rage. The pain and anger I felt only ate the more of me up, just like it always had and always would. The curse's grip on me was undeniable. It had taken hold of me like a cancer and it was terminal. There was no cure and there was definitely no hope for me. If I had no hope for myself then who would? I staggered to my feet and looked back at the grate. I just wanted to finish what I had come to do and leave this place. I was about to go, when I heard the sound of sobbing. More ghosts, I feared.

"I'm sorry, Momma," the voice pleaded.

I spun around and spied through the trees to see Melody being dragged through the woods by her mother.

"Please, Momma!" Melody cried out, trying to pull herself free of her mother's grip.

"Shut your evil mouth!" her mother barked. "I don't want to hear the devil talking to me."

"No, Momma," Melody begged. She stumbled forward and over into the leaf-covered ground. Her bonnet came free, and I staggered backwards. Melody's head had been shaved. Gone was her pink hair. Melody was dragged, kicking and screaming, into a small clearing.

Springing into the air, I became the monster which lurked inside of me and raced towards them. From a nearby tree, I watched her momma snatch up the fallen bonnet. Melody lay at her momma's feet sobbing.

"Please let me go, Momma," she begged, lacing her fingers together as if in prayer.

"Don't speak to me," her mother hissed, pulling the black cords free of the bonnet she held in her hands. "It is my daughter's lips that move, but the devil's voice I can hear."

"Please..." Melody started. But her last word was strangled into nothing as her mother wrapped the cord from the bonnet around her daughter's throat.

Melody threw her hands into the air and clawed at her neck. It felt odd watching Melody and her mother struggle together – it was like watching two nuns having a fight. Melody kicked her legs out as her mother forced her flat onto the ground. I stuck my long snout around the edge of the tree, my eyes blazing almost red. I wanted to lunge from my hiding place and stop this. I wanted to save Melody.

Don't change anything... I heard Lilly Blu whisper in my ear.

So it was the mother who killed Melody Rose and I had to just sit back and watch that happen. Was this some kind of punishment for all the lives I had taken... was this in some way to illustrate to me the futility of killing?

With my heart racing in my chest, and fighting the unbearable urge to stop Melody from being strangled to death, I slipped back behind the tree before I was seen. I lay on my front, giant paws over my ears, as I tried to block out the sound of Melody gasping and fighting for air. I could hear her hands slapping against her mother, and her feet thrashing against the leaves as she fought for her life. After what seemed like an eternity, the sounds of Melody's fight began to lessen until they finally stopped. Peering around the edge of the tree, I watched Melody's mother climb off her daughter's lifeless body. She looked down at Melody, and lacing her fingers together she silently prayed.

The urge to bound into the clearing and rip the woman to pieces was almost too much to bear. I wanted to kill this woman more than I'd ever wanted to kill anyone. But I knew I couldn't. However much agony Melody's mother had caused, I was unable to do anything about it – just like I had been unable to prevent it. I heard the sound of rustling and looked back around the tree. The mother was heading out of the clearing, leaving Melody's body on the ground amongst the fallen leaves and twigs. Once her mother had gone, I crept into the clearing. Rearing up on my back legs, I changed back into my human form.

Melody lay outstretched on the ground before me. One hand clutched her purple and bloated face. Her lips were blue, and her tongue snaked from the corner of her mouth looking black and bloated. Melody's knees were drawn up where she had kicked out wildly with her legs. The hem of her dress had been hitched up, revealing her tattoo-covered thighs. I knelt down beside her, and lowering her skirt to cover her legs, I gently took her into my arms.

Memories of how I'd cradled my own dead sister, Kara, in my arms crashed over me. Throwing my head back, I howled in agony and despair. I had never felt so much pain and sorrow. It was like the pain of all my victims eating away at my black heart. Melody hadn't deserved to die, nor had my sister and neither had any of my victims. With bright golden tears streaming from my eyes and down the length of my gaunt face, I howled and howled. I held Melody's shaven head against my chest, my body racked with gut-wrenching sobs.

Very gently, I lay her back on the ground. I folded Melody's hands over her chest and closed the lids over her bulging eyes. I heard the sound of approaching footfalls amongst the leaves. I sprang to my feet to see Melody's mother approaching, carrying a spade in her hand. I headed back out of the clearing. I looked back just once more at Melody lying dead on the ground. Her mother stood over her dead daughter's body and placed the blade of the spade against Melody's neck. Then, lifting her foot, she stomped down on the spade, cutting off Melody's head.

My first thought was of Isi-bore and I guessed he would be frantically looking for Melody by now. Did he know that she had been taken by her mother? Perhaps, but I doubted he knew where Melody had been taken. If Isi-bore did know, then I figured he would be in the woods already. I headed down to the shore by the lake. I checked out the bush Melody and Is-bore had spent so much time in together. He wasn't there. Perhaps he had gone back into The Hollows, but I doubted it. I made my way along the shore, then in the distance I saw him talking to the boy he had argued with a few days before. Crouching low, I watched them talk, although I couldn't hear what was being said. It didn't look like they were arguing this time around. After a short conversation, I saw Isi-bore run away from the other boy in the direction of town.

I followed at a distance and I knew that he was heading for Melody's home. The sun was starting to fade as the day grew gradually to a close. Isidor pushed open the front gate and raced up the garden path. I could see no sign of the mother's car, and I guessed she was still burying her daughter in the woods. I wanted to leap from the bushes and tell Isi-bore he was in the wrong place, I wanted to tell him where he would find the body of the girl he loved, but I couldn't. I wasn't meant to change anything, I reminded myself.

Isi-bore yanked on the front door and it rattled in its frame. Discovering it was locked, he went around the side of the house. I waited several minutes to see if he would come back. When he didn't, I snuck from my hiding place. I bounded over the wall and then looked back at the dirt track as the sound of an approaching car could be heard from the distance. Bent double, I crept around the side of the house and dropped over the stone wall, where the window led into the basement. I peered inside to see Isi-bore.

At first I thought I startled him, as he jerked his head up. But he didn't turn to face the window. Just like me, Isi-bore had heard the sound of the car approaching, and both of us knew it was

Melody's mother. But instead of running like I thought he would, Isi-bore headed over to the large cross and stood in the shadows before the altar. There was a metal chain, and pulling on it, he hoisted himself up, so it looked as if he had been crucified. I heard the car door slam, the sound of the mother's shoes crunching over gravel as she made her way up to the front door. It opened then closed.

On all fours, I pressed my face against the grubby window. Melody's mother came down the stairs and into the basement where Isi-bore was hiding. At the bottom stair, she lit two candles and placed these before a small font made of stone. She raised her hands in prayer and I saw blood drip from them. Very carefully, I eased the window open just an inch with my fingertips. The mother plunged her hands into the water in the font and washed the blood from between her fingers. Once she had washed the evidence of what she had done away, she dropped to her knees and began to pray.

"Dear Lord, I have sent my wretched child to you for forgiveness. Please release her of her demons, if that is your will."

She's got to be fucking joking, right? Melody had no demons in her. I knew all about living with demons.

"Dear sweet Jesus, I pray that you reward me now that I have carried out your will... now that Melody is dead," she said.

And I thought I was fucked in the head! There were no rewards for people like me and her.

I saw a dark shadow fall over her upturned face. At first I did believe that the devil had truly come to take her. Two giant black wings fluttered across my eye line as Isi-bore flew down from the cross.

"Don't look," he demanded. "You're not fit to look upon me."

Melody's mother cried out in fear and dropped to the floor.

Was Isi-bore finally going to let his monster free and rip this bitch's fucking head off? Part of me hoped not.

"What did you do?" he asked, fluttering in the shadows so she couldn't see his face.

"What the Lord asked me to do," the woman moaned. "I

killed the demon within my child by sacrificing her."

Isi-bore dropped to the floor and raced across the chapel towards Melody's mother. His wings were spread open on either side of him. He took hold of the woman, dragging her roughly to her feet.

"Are you an angel?" she asked, her eyes wide with fear.

She fucking hoped he was.

"It's not me who is the angel!" he screamed at her. "It was your daughter, and you will burn in Hell for what you have done to her!"

"No!" the woman wailed. She dropped to the floor where she began to cover Isi-bore's feet with kisses. "I beg you... please, you must forgive me."

"There is no forgiveness for what you have done," he told her. And like me, she knew what Isi-bore had said was true.

Isi-bore kicked her away, as if her very touch revolted him. Melody's mother began to sob hysterically on the floor. But I knew she wasn't crying for forgiveness for what she had done, she was crying for herself.

From my hiding place, I watched Isi-bore stumble out into the fields that stretched away at the back of the house. He dropped to his knees like he had been shot. Keeping low, I made my way through the long, overgrown grass. I watched with a heavy heart as he pounded the ground with his fists over and over again.

He looked up into the heavens and screamed. *"I hate you!"*

Tears streamed down his face and I saw myself as a boy again, hiding in the shadows at the back of the church as Father Paul's coffin was carried in. I could feel the hot tears streaming down my face, and gnawed on my own fist to prevent myself from screaming. I watched Isidor race up into the sky, the roar of his grief sounding like thunder.

Why hadn't he taken revenge for Melody's death? Why hadn't he murdered her mother? Because Isidor was a fighter, not a killer. But I was a killer, and I knew I could never change. The curse – the monster inside of me – would never be beaten.

Finally admitting this to myself, I headed back towards the house. Isidor might not be able to kill the bitch, but I could.

Chapter Twenty-Eight

Potter

It was cold along the desolate track. The wind blew down from the hills and screamed through the branches of the nearby trees. I guess if Sparky had planned to kill Kiera tonight, he couldn't have chosen a better location. Even though the night sky was clear of cloud, it was still so dark at times that it was near impossible to see just a few yards ahead. By torchlight, Sparky gave me and Kiera something close to a briefing. He had all the intel about this operation written down in his police notebook. Sparky explained he had received information that the ATM at Bleak Point Station was going to be hit.

"Who was the source of information?" I asked him.

"Just an informant I've been using over the last few months or so," he said, eyeing me. How long was he going to keep up this pretence of not knowing that I was six feet under somewhere?

"What was their name?" I pushed.

"That's classified information," he said back.

"Classified information?" I smiled at Kiera. Then, looking back at Sparky, I added, "C'mon, we're all coppers here. You can tell us your secrets."

"I've never actually spoken to this person. Whoever the informant is, he sends me the information in short handwritten messages," he said, pushing his crooked glasses up onto the bridge of his nose. "It's a trust thing between me and my informant."

"So you don't trust us?" I asked.

"Hey, c'mon, Potter," Kiera said, placing a hand gently on my arm. "We're all on the same side."

"Are we?" I muttered, glancing at Sparky in the darkness.

He ignored my comment and went back to thumbing through his notebook. "My informant has told me that the team planning this robbery are going to reverse a flatbed truck through the doors of the station. They will then attach chains to the rear of

174

the truck and then wrap these around the ATM. They will drive off at speed, ripping the ATM free from its housing, taking the ATM with them."

"So they're a sophisticated crew?" I sighed. "They sound like just a bunch of chain snatching punks."

"Despite what you think, Potter," Sparky said, "this so-called bunch of chain snatchers have stolen over five hundred thousand pounds by committing robberies in the past few months. If you think this is beneath you, then perhaps you should go back to special operations on 'C' Division."

"Ever worked on 'C' Division yourself?" I asked, staring straight back at him.

He didn't flinch at my question. "Once or twice," he smiled.

"Hey, you two," Kiera said. "We're meant to be a team here."

"So you keep saying," I said, turning away.

There was a short silence as if to give everyone a short breather to gather their thoughts and let the icy atmosphere defrost a little.

"So what time are we expecting the Brady Bunch to show up?" I asked, looking back over my shoulder at Sparky and Kiera.

Sparky shone his torch at his wristwatch and said, "At midnight. We have about an hour."

"So what's the plan?" Kiera asked, her eagerness to catch some bad guys as strong as the day she had walked into the Ragged Cove Police Station in the world before it was *pushed*.

We head up the hill from here to the station," Sparky explained. "We leave our cars here."

"And what if they make off in their van, how do we expect to catch them?" I asked, deliberately looking for holes in his plan.

"I dunno?" Sparky shrugged. "Perhaps you could fly, Potter?"

"What's that s'posed to mean?" I shot right back. Was he testing me?

"It was just a joke," Sparky said with a smile.

"Stop being so tetchy," Kiera said, curling her hand around mine in the darkness and lovingly squeezing my fingers.

"I'm not being tetchy…"

"Yes, you are. Relax," she smiled.

How could I relax knowing that Sparky – the guy she trusted to be her friend – was setting her up just like he had once before? But she didn't remember that. That had been a different Kiera.

"Let's get going," Sparky said, eager to set off up the hill.

We followed him in silence, Kiera not letting go of my hand once as we made our way to the remote railway station. Halfway up the hill we came across the railway tracks and we followed them. Sparky insisted that we kept off the road, just in case the robbers were watching the station before they struck.

We followed the tracks as they snaked towards the station ahead of us in the dark. I could just make out its squat-looking shape in the distance. We walked in silence, the only sound was the wind rustling in the nearby undergrowth that grew up alongside the railway tracks. Arriving at the station, we climbed up onto the single platform. Crouched low, we followed Sparky to the waiting room. There was a glass-front ticket office and I half expected to see Noah sitting behind it waiting to punch out some tickets. But the ticket office was in darkness, and over the glass hung a sign which read CLOSED. There were a couple of wooden benches and in one corner there was the ATM. On the other side of the waiting room were the glass doors the robbers were going to apparently reverse their vehicle into and snatch the machine.

Speaking just above a whisper, Sparky leant in close and said, "Kiera, have you got your radio?"

"Yes," she whispered back, taking it from her pocket.

"Okay," he said, taking his own radio from inside his jacket and switching it on. There was a crackle of static. "What about you?"

"What about me?" I asked.

"Got your radio?"

"Nope," I shrugged.

"Okay," he said. "Kiera, you go round to the front of the station. There is a small cycle shed for you to hide in. From it, you'll have a good view of the road. When you see the van approach, call me on the radio, then me and Potter will get ready…"

"What's this 'me and you'?" I asked. "I'm staying close to Kiera."

"No, I need you in here with me," he hushed.

"Why?"

"Because when they reverse that van through those doors and climb from the van to attach the chains to the ATM, I want you with me to help, as I suspect they're gonna want to fight."

"I'm good in a fight, too," Kiera cut in.

"I know you are, but that's not what I mean," Sparky said. Then, glancing at me, he said, "Besides, it will give me and Potter a chance to catch up. I'm sure we've got a lot to talk about."

I looked at him, then at Kiera. "Perhaps he's right, Kiera," I said. "I'd like to have a catch-up with my old friend Sparky, too."

Kiera screwed up her eyes and shot me a distrustful look. She knew I didn't like Sparky. Then sighing, she said, "Okay, have it your way, the both of you. But I've come to stop a robbery taking place tonight, not a bitch fight between you two."

Turning away, Kiera headed out of the waiting room to take up her post in the cycle shed at the front of the station.

Once she had gone, and me and Sparky were alone, I looked at him and said, "Why don't you cut the crap. You know I'm fucking dead."

"Dead?" Sparky frowned. "Is this some kinda joke?"

"There's only one fucking joke around here, Sparky, and I'm looking right at him," I spat. "Now stop trying to jerk me off and start talking."

With a deep sigh, Sparky sat down on one of the benches. "I don't even know where to start."

I could see that he was trembling.

He raised his head to look at me and said, "I'm a wolf…"

"No shit, Sherlock. Tell me something I don't know," I barked at him.

"I'm not like the other wolves," he said. "I'm better than them."

"Bullshit," I spat. "All wolves are the same. Filthy killers. And you killed me."

"I didn't kill you, Potter," he said, wringing his hands together.

"Who did?" I barked, my patience fast running out.

"All I know is that you were killed by a wolf, but I don't know who," he said.

"Look, you ain't no good to me if you don't know anything, so I might as well kill you now," I said, taking a step closer to him.

"I know you're not the Potter who got murdered," he said, raising his hands as if to protect himself. "I know you've come from another *place* – if that's the right word."

"Who told you this?" I demanded.

"The one who calls himself the Wolf Man," Sparky said, dropping his voice to a whisper again. "He has some kind of special interest in Kiera. He sent me to watch her and to report back to him. But… but…"

"But what?" I said, yanking him up off the bench.

"I fell in love with her," he confessed, unable to match my stare.

"And that's why you killed me, because you wanted Kiera all to yourself," I said, gripping him around the throat.

"No… you're wrong…" he gasped.

I loosened my grip just an inch, so he could talk more freely.

"I was just as surprised that you walked out on Kiera as she was," Sparky said. "You were madly in love with her… you would have done anything for Kiera. But I thought perhaps the Wolf Man had gotten to you – scared you away. But then your body turned up. It was ripped to pieces. It was obvious you had been murdered by a wolf."

"So if I was taken out of the picture, why did you have to keep spying on Kiera?" I breathed into his face.

"Because the Wolf Man was convinced that even though you were dead, you might show up again in Kiera's life," Sparky struggled to explain. "I never really believed the Wolf Man. I didn't think it could be possible. But he was right. I don't know how or by what magic, but you have come back, Potter."

I started to believe that he didn't really understand that the world had been *pushed*. I loosened my grip on him a little more. "So if you love Kiera so much, why have you set her up to die here tonight?" I snarled just an inch from his face.

"It isn't Kiera I have set up to die here tonight," Sparky wheezed, around my grip on his throat. "It's you, Potter. Kiera met me for dinner the other night and told me that you had come back from 'C' Division. I never told her you were murdered. I loved her too much to cause her that pain. So when she told me that you were back... well, you can imagine what I must have been thinking. Kiera was too upset to eat, so she left for home. It was then I contacted the Wolf Man and told him you had returned, just like he feared you would one day."

"You haven't changed," I hissed, pushing him back down onto the bench. "You always were a fucking coward and a snake."

"You make it sound like you once knew me in another time... another *place*," he said, his eyes round and full of fear.

"Don't you mean another *where* and *when*?" I sneered.

"So my dreams... my nightmares are true," he whispered. "They're memories I'm having. I dreamt that I was a killer... tell me, Potter, what was I really like?"

"Honestly?" I said, looking at him.

"Yes," he nodded.

"You were nothing but a piece of shit," I said. "But the funny thing is, this Wolf Man who you have put your trust in, was known by another name. In that *where* and *when* he was called Luke Bishop and he murdered you!"

"But..." Sparky said, getting up.

I pushed him back down onto the bench. "So is this Wolf Man coming here to kill me tonight?" I breathed.

"No, he is sending another wolf to kill you," Sparky said.

"Who?" I demanded to know.

Before Sparky had a chance to answer, there was a bang, sounding like a small explosion. His head snapped backwards, his brains jetting from the back of his head and splattering against the waiting room wall like a lump of raw steak. Sparky jerked, as if

179

having a violent spasm, then fell into my arms.

There was another shot followed by the sound of Kiera screaming.

"Kiera!" I roared.

Chapter Twenty-Nine

Jack

Melody's mother was lying prostrate on the chapel floor when I snuck through the window. Her deafening sobs drowned the sound of my approach. Unbeknown to her, I sat silently for some time on one of the pews and watched her cry and beg for forgiveness. She was pathetic. I started to chuckle at the thought of what I had planned for her. It was the sound of my laughing that finally made her stop sobbing and look up at me. Discovering Uncle Jack watching her from out of the gloom, she screamed, scrambling backwards across the chapel floor.

"Shhh..." I cooed with a grin.

I could read the fear in her eyes and I felt that twinge of excitement I always felt at this point.

"Your eyes," she murmured. "I have seen eyes like yours before."

"Have you, indeed," I asked with genuine curiosity.

"The devil who put his seed in me had eyes just like yours," she whispered, her face taut with terror. "Melody's father was a devil just like you."

"How like me?" I said, slinking from the pew and dropping onto all fours. I crawled slowly towards her, my eyes blazing bright.

"He was a wolf," she murmured, staring back into my eyes. "He was the devil."

So Melody's father was a wolf. That's why her mother hated her – feared her – so much. That's why she took Melody's head off with a spade. She feared strangulation wasn't enough. The only sure way of killing a wolf was by cutting off its head. I thought of my brother Nik kneeling over the guillotine and I knew in my heart he was dead forever.

"Keep away from me," she sobbed.

"Don't you like what you see in my eyes?" I snarled. "Does it excite you?"

"Yes..." she whispered, her face haggard-looking with fright.

"Good," I smiled, crawling towards her, my long, sharp fingernails scrapping across the cold stone floor. "Me and you are going to have so much fun."

Just before dawn, and after more fun than I'd had in a very long time, I took the chains which hung from the cross. And just like the bonnet cord she had used to strangle her daughter, I wrapped the chains around momma's throat. At first I think she thought it was just another one of the many depraved games I'd had her taking part in over the last few hours as I hung her from beneath the stairs which led out of the basement.

But as her eyes bulged in their wrinkled sockets and her tongue shot out of her mouth, she knew the fun and games had finally come to an end. And so had she. Stepping back into my jeans, I got dressed and went upstairs to the kitchen. And after cooking and eating a breakfast of bacon, eggs, and toast, I left the house and didn't look back. I knew my time here was nearly over and I was glad about that. I'd had enough.

I crept through the woods and towards the grate. Isidor was standing and looking down at it, a look of puzzlement etched across his face. He then bent down and took something that had been wedged between the metal bars.

I didn't have to get a clearer view to know that it was the photograph of him and Melody he had just found. I had missed the photographer! Could he or she still be close by? I wondered, looking back over my shoulder. How was I going to go back without unmasking the photographer? What would this mean for the world I'd come from? What would this mean for my sister Kiera? I'd fucked up. I'd been too busy having fun with Melody's mother when I should have been here, in the woods, watching the grate. Perhaps Potter had had more luck? Maybe his mission had been more successful?

Isi-bore placed the picture inside his coat and climbed down into the hole. I crept from my hiding place. Standing over the hole, I peered down into the darkness. There was a sound behind me. It was the sound of feet running over fallen leaves. I spun around to see a figure, its face concealed behind a grey coloured hoody. A camera swung about the figure's neck. Before I could get out of the way, the photographer pushed me hard in the chest and I stumbled backwards into the hole that led down into The Hollows. I clattered into the sides of the tunnel. Over and over I went as I raced towards the bottom. The tunnel became darker and darker until everything went black.

I hit the ground with a thud and opened my eyes. I was outside. There was a storm raging. Heavy black clouds lumbered across the sky. Dawn wasn't far off.

Where was I? Was I back?

I stood up in the hammering rain. There was a building a short distance away. I looked down and could see I was standing in the middle of a set of railway tracks. Had the train brought me back? I couldn't be sure. I set off in the direction of the building. I was in a valley. *Where* and *when*, I couldn't be sure. Even before I reached the small wooden structure, I knew what it was. It was another freaking railway station. Perhaps I was back after all. Reaching the platform, I climbed on to it. Over the sound of the wind and the rain, I could hear voices. I crept along the platform, stopping outside a small waiting room. Very carefully, so as not to be seen, I peered through one of the windows. I stepped backwards almost at once and into the shadows again. Gathered inside the waiting room was Kiera, Potter, Kayla, Isi-bore, and a teenage boy was sleeping on one of the benches. I couldn't be back from where I started from, I figured, my mind racing. Potter was here, but so was Kiera. Kiera thought Potter was dead where I had come from.

Then I heard Kiera say, "Have you still got that photograph?"

I peered back through the window to see Isi-bore reach inside his coat pocket and pull out a folded piece of paper. I knew it was the picture the photographer had left for him in the grate.

I heard Isi-bore explain that after Melody's death he would often go back above ground and visit the lake where he had spent so many happy hours with her. But going back became too painful. In the end he stopped going above ground.

"Did you never go back again?" I heard Potter ask.

"I only went back once more, and that time, I went to the house where she had lived with her mum," Isi-bore explained. "The windows were all boarded over. The front garden was overgrown with weeds and wildflowers. The house looked derelict and abandoned. I wanted to know what had happened, so I returned to the library and checked the local newspapers. I didn't have to look for very long, as I soon came across an article about a local woman who had hung herself in a chapel constructed in the basement of her house."

I turned away from the window and leant against the waiting room wall. Somehow I had been *pushed* forward.

I glanced to my right and saw Kayla looking out of the window. I crouched down, out of sight.

"What's wrong?" I heard Kiera ask.

"I can hear them coming," Kayla said.

"Hear who?" Potter asked.

"Those berserkers, and there's a lot of them," Kayla gasped.

I squinted and peered into the darkness that covered the valley like a thick blanket. Then, I realised that it wasn't shadows at all but a wave of Berserkers racing into the valley and towards the station.

From inside the waiting room, I heard snippets of conversation as the group planned to make their escape. Suddenly the waiting room door was flung open and Potter appeared in the open doorway. Pressing myself flat against the wall of the station, I edged my way a little further along the platform.

"A train is coming," I heard Kayla say.

"The train is close, but so are those berserkers," Potter snapped, racing back into the waiting room. I could hear him barking his orders at the others.

It was then I heard Isi-bore, say, "Kiera, I'm not coming with you."

"Listen, kid, we don't have time to fuck about. Get your shit together, we're moving out!" Potter yelled at him.

"I'm not coming," Isi-bore said again.

From within the shadows, I listened to the others as they pleaded with Isi-bore to go with them.

I looked out across the valley and could see the Berserkers drawing nearer. Their barking and howling added to the deafening boom of the thunder and sizzling lightning overhead. Isi-bore was still insisting that his friends left without him.

Run! Run! Isidor, I felt like screaming myself. He didn't need to die – not today and not at the hands of the Berserkers. I dared to glance back through the waiting room window. Isidor was smiling at his sister, just like how I'd seen him smile at Melody Rose.

"You go," Isidor told Kayla. "I'll stay and draw them away so you can escape."

Run, Isidor! I howled inside as the Berserkers grew ever closer. In the direction I had come from, I could see the headlamp of an approaching train. I looked back through the window. Kayla and Potter were both now pleading with Isidor to go with them. Knowing that they were fast running out of time, Potter helped Kayla drag the unconscious-looking boy out onto the platform. I stepped back into the doorway of the station bathroom. Potter and Kayla passed by me, dragging the boy between them. The train drew nearer, as did the Berserkers.

I then heard Isidor say something that made my twisted black heart stop.

"I have to stay and wait for Melody," Isidor said.

"But the berserkers will kill you while you wait for her," I heard Kiera try and reason with him.

"But don't you see?" Isidor said. "The berserkers can't kill me because this picture hasn't been taken yet. The fact that it exists says that I'm not going to die today."

Isidor was going to die because I failed to intercept the picture. I had been too busy enjoying myself with Melody's mother. If I'd only beaten my lust to kill for a few hours, then

Isidor would now be escaping with his friends.

"I'm so tired of waiting – hoping that the moment this picture was taken comes," he said. "So maybe by waiting for the berserkers, it will force her hand and she'll come for me."

Melody isn't going to come for you! I felt like screaming. It's a fucking trap, you dumb-arse!

"I love you, Isidor," I heard Kiera say. "See you later, alligator," she added before running from the waiting room and leaving her friend behind. From my hiding place in the dark, I couldn't help but see the tears streaming down Kiera's face as she dashed past me along the platform. I could see her pain. And I knew in my heart that the pain hadn't been caused by the Elders – it had been caused by me because I hadn't been able to stop killing – not for one single hour. I had failed to unmask the photographer and Isidor was going to die because of that.

Her parting words to Isidor rang in my ears as loud as the thunder and the roaring Berserkers.

I love you, she had said.

No one had ever said those words to me. Not ever. And I knew no one ever would. I was unlovable and I had chosen to be so. No one else was to blame.

Kiera stood crying on the platform, her arms wrapped around Kayla. Potter strode past me and back into the waiting room. The train was clearly visible now in the distance, as were the Berserkers as they raced towards the station.

"Why are you doing this?" I heard Potter ask Isidor.

"Because I want to see Melody again," he answered.

I glanced at Kiera and Kayla, both had their backs to me, so I snuck out from my hiding place and positioned myself in the shadows by the door of the waiting room.

"I'm staying, Potter, I know what I'm doing," Isidor said.

What with the sound of the approaching train, the raging storm, and the howling Berserkers, I struggled to hear whatever it was Potter said to Isidor.

I then saw something I didn't ever expect to see. Potter walked forward and hugged Isidor tightly in his arms. He then placed a cigarette behind Isidor's ear. Potter then turned and didn't look back.

As Potter raced up the platform to his friends, the train pulled into the station. Looking back over my shoulder at the approaching Berserkers, I knew they would be swarming over the station in just a minute or two. I took my chance and snuck into the waiting room.

"Jack Seth?" Isidor breathed, on seeing me.

"Give me the picture," I barked at him.

"No," he said. "It's mine."

I lunged for it, snatching it from his hand. I tore it into strips and cast them to the floor.

"That was a picture of Mel..." he started.

"I know what it was, numb-nuts," I snarled. "And it isn't what you think it is. It's a trap!"

"What has this got to do with you?" Isidor said, raising his crossbow. "You're my enemy."

Knocking the crossbow from his hand with a swipe of my claws, I dragged one hooked fingernail down his chest. A gash opened up in his flesh and Isidor cried out.

"Don't be such a fucking cry-baby the whole time," I warned him, dipping my finger in the blood that now trickled from his chest.

He watched me with a look of disgust as I sucked his blood from my finger. I lurched forward, clutching my guts as I started to change.

"What's happening?" Isidor gasped as I took on his form before him.

"I'm saving your fucking life, that's what's happening," I said, as his blood mixed with mine and I became him. "Jeezus, Isidor, your head really is full of dumb fucking ideas."

"Why are you doing this?" he asked, a look of bewilderment on his face.

"Because I want you to go and find your friend, Melody Rose," I told him, glancing back at the door. "She'll be waiting for you, trust me." The Berserkers were now climbing up and over the platform. The train was gaining speed as it cleared the station.

Turning to look at Isidor, I said, "Hide! Get under the bench and don't come out until it's safe to do so."

"What are you going to do?" Isidor asked, dropping to the floor.

"I'm going to let them kill me," I said, crossing the waiting room and closing the door. And just for a moment, I saw a brief reflection of myself. For once I didn't look emaciated and haggard; I looked young and full of hope. I looked like Isidor.

The Berserkers leapt onto the platform. They sniffed the air and snarled. They saw me looking at them through the glass. I turned around. Isidor was hidden out of sight beneath the bench.

"Why are you doing this for me?" I heard Isidor whisper from beneath the bench.

"Because you will go on to do great things, Isidor," I whispered back. "Whereas, I will only go on to kill."

There was a vacant-looking ticket booth. On the counter I saw an old-fashioned radio, just like Melody had bought to the lake.

"Let's have some music," I smiled, switching it on. There was the sound of static. I shook the radio and I could hear the distant sound of music. The door to the waiting room opened, and I didn't need to look back to know that the Berserkers were creeping up behind me, their razor-sharp teeth glistening wetly and their giant claws raised.

The music from the radio grew louder, drowning out the sound of my approaching executioners. I recognised the song at once. It was *Heroes* by David Bowie – the same song that Melody and Isidor used to listen to together on the shore. The music grew so loud that it was almost deafening. The walls of the waiting room began to vibrate. I noticed some leavers set into the wall. Written above them were the words *PUSH* and *PULL*.

I felt the first of the Berserkers claws rip at my throat. I gripped one of the levers, and do you know what I did next? I *pushed* harder than I'd ever fucking *pushed* before.

I felt a hand fall over mine and take hold. I staggered forward

188

and someone caught me in their arms. Their embrace felt familiar. I leant back and looked into my brother's face.

He grinned at me.

"Good to see you, Nik," I smiled.

"And you, brother," he said.

I looked over his shoulder and could see that I was in a railway station, similar to the one I'd just left. There were a few tables with people seated at them. Bright sunlight streamed through the windows and I walked towards it. I pushed open the wooden station door. The sun beat down on a flat and arid-looking wasteland. There was a squeaking noise from overhead. I glanced up to a see a sign swinging slowly back and forth in the breeze. It read:

Welcome to the Great Wasteland Railroad

Nik joined me in the bright, hot sun. I took off my bandana and wiped sweat from my brow.

"We're dead, aren't we?" I said, looking out across the vast desert.

"We had our heads cut off, didn't we?" he said, looking at me.

"We sure did," I said.

Tumbleweed blew along the rickety platform that we stood on.

"What now?" Nik asked me.

"We start again, I guess," I said. Then turning to face him, I added, "But this time, can we try and be heroes and not monsters?"

"I like the sound of that," Nik said with a happy smile.

Chapter Thirty

Potter

I heard another blast of gunfire. Pushing Sparky's corpse off me, I raced to the front of the station. Through the glass doors, I peered out into the night. Kiera screamed again, and I saw her run from the cycle shed. Another spray of gunfire, and bullets whizzed all around Kiera as she desperately tried to make her escape. Taking a step backwards, I then launched myself through the glass front doors of the station. Shards of glass showered up into the night sky and glinted like ice. I landed on the ground, my wings out, claws raised. I brandished my fangs as I scanned the darkness for whoever was trying to shoot Kiera.

Clack! Clack! Clack!

Another scream from Kiera, this time from the rear of the station. With my wings pointed out behind me, I shot into the air and soared over the roof of the station. I could see Kiera running across the fields back towards where we had left the cars. Swooping out of the sky, I took hold of her around the waist.

She screamed again – this time with surprise.

"Hold tight," I whispered into her ear, launching myself back into the night sky with Kiera in my arms.

Clack! Clack! Clack!

Bullets screamed past us as I corkscrewed through the air. Glancing back at the ground, I tried to get a look at the gunman, but I couldn't see him. I would get Kiera to safety then come back in search of him. Kiera tightened her arms about me as I raced through the air, my wings rippling on either side of me. She pressed her face against my chest and I glanced down at her to make sure she was okay. She looked up into my eyes, and they were bright. I didn't know if they shone so brightly with fear or excitement. Her long, black hair billowed out behind her in the wind. Kiera looked beautiful, and in a strange way, it was kinda like falling in love with her all over again.

190

Soaring over the hills, the cold night air pulling at us, I swooped down and towards the hidden dirt track where Kiera and Sparky had left their cars. I wanted Kiera to get as far away from here as quickly as possible. With my feet touching the ground, I slowly lifted Kiera out of my arms. She stood and held onto me.

Looking up into my face, she whispered, "So it is true, there are winged creatures. You're one of them."

So are you, I desperately wanted to say. I couldn't – I had done too much – changed too much already. I had stopped Kiera from getting shot and killed tonight. How much that would change, I didn't know, and at this point in time, I didn't much care. Kiera was safe, and that's all that mattered to me.

Still in my arms, she reached out and tentatively touched one of my tatty-looking wings with her fingertips. "They're beautiful," she whispered as if waking from a dream.

"Kiera..." I started.

"Shhh," she said, placing her lips over mine.

Her lips felt warm and soft. She pulled me close, and I felt her against me. Kiera's kiss became more passionate. I tried to ease myself from her, but she snaked one hand around the nape of my neck and kissed me harder. Her tongue slipped into my mouth, and my heart raced. I closed my eyes, then opened them almost at once. There was something wrong. The underside of Kiera's tongue was covered in silky fine hair.

I pushed her back from me. I looked into her eyes and they were ablaze with orange light. It looked as if there was a fire raging inside her skull. "Kiera...?" I whispered, looking at her.

"Yes," she smiled.

Then thinking of how I'd been deceived by female wolves before, I said, "You can't be Kiera. This is a trick... you've got to be... *Lilly!*" I hissed.

"Who's Lilly?" Kiera said, tilting her head to one side and staring at me with her bright yellow eyes. "Not another woman?"

"What other woman?" I mumbled, trying to play catch-up. If this was another one of Seth's mind-fucks, he was dead.

"I knew there were others," Kiera said. "But that's not why I killed you."

"Killed me...?" I breathed, looking at her. "Kiera, what are you talking about?"

"I had to prove that I wasn't the other Kiera," she smiled, her long, black hair seeming to grow thicker somehow as it blew in the wind.

"Prove what to who?" This had to be a Jack Seth mind-fuck. "Am I being punked here, or what? What are you talking about, Kiera?" Had she lost her fucking mind?

"The Wolf Man told me that if I still wanted to hunt with the wolves – to be one of them – I had to prove I wasn't the Dead Angel the wolves feared was going to come and destroy them. The Wolf Man said I had the same name as her – that I was identical to her – that he was going to kill me. I begged for my life. But how could I prove that I wasn't this other Kiera Hudson the Wolf Man spoke of? So he asked me to kill my lover – to kill you, Potter. He said the real Kiera Hudson would give up her own life to save yours."

"So you killed me – you killed the other Potter," I said, the pieces of the puzzle clanking together like a boxful of spanners in my mind.

"I ripped his fucking face off and ate his heart while the Wolf Man watched," Kiera said, a sly smile playing on her red lips. "Only then did he believe that I wasn't the Kiera Hudson – the *Dead Angel* – he was waiting for.

"But you're half Vampyrus... you have wings like me, Kiera," I said, my heart feeling like she had just ripped it from my chest. But in my heart, which now felt so heavy, I knew she was also half wolf. In this *pushed* world, Kiera was more wolf than Vampyrus. Lilly and the little girl had been right – this wasn't *my* Kiera. She looked like her – sounded like her – but she wasn't her. I started to walk backwards, putting some distance between us.

"So those lumps are wings then?" Kiera asked, looking revolted by the idea. "That's what the Wolf Man thought when he saw them. And even though I had killed my lover in front of him, the Wolf Man once again started to believe that I was really this Dead Angel, he so feared. And just when I thought he might kill me once and for all, you showed up in my apartment and I realised I had another chance to prove that I was truly a wolf and have no love for you."

No sooner had the last of her words passed over her lips Kiera had sprung into the air. As she leapt towards me, her body changed into the form of a giant black wolf. Kiera's body was now long and sleek, her face wolf-like and pointed with a vicious-looking snout. The black fur that now covered her body glistened in the moonlight.

"No, Kiera!" I roared, leaping out of her way.

She hit the ground, her long, bushy black tail whipping to and fro as she turned to face me again.

"Don't make me kill you, Kiera," I said, tears standing in my eyes.

"You won't kill me," she snarled. "You can't kill me because you love me. The Wolf Man was right. The love you and this other Kiera Hudson have for each other will be what kills you."

Kiera bounded towards me, and swiping one giant claw through the air, she cut four jagged tears across my chest. I pushed her back and cried out in pain.

"Don't listen to this Wolf Man," I tried to reason with her. "He isn't who or what you think he is."

Kiera leapt at me again, her eyes bright and full of rage. I rolled back my fist and punched her straight in the snout. Yelping and howling, she flew backwards into the side of her little red Mini. Scrambling onto all fours, Kiera looked back at me as she leapt onto the roof of the car. "He told me to bring you up here tonight and kill you. If I did that, then I would be free."

"He doesn't have the faintest fucking idea what true freedom is!" I roared at her. To see Kiera like this was agony. "He isn't a wolf. He's a Vampyrus like me, and he wants to rule you. He wants to rule everyone. That isn't freedom."

"Liar!" she howled, leaping from the car at me.

I dropped, and raising my claws into the air, I dragged them down the side of her body. I could of driven my claws deep inside her – killed her – but I couldn't. I didn't have it in me to kill Kiera. I knew there would be good inside of her. There had to be – she was Kiera Hudson.

"Kiera, listen to me," I shouted, as she rolled over in the dirt. She was panting heavily now as blood gushed from her side, matting her black fur together. "The Wolf Man is called Luke Bishop or Elias Munn… he has many names and faces… but one thing for sure is that he will kill you."

"Why?" she snarled.

"Because the other Kiera Hudson… the Kiera I love… she won't ever give up the fight. She won't ever be beaten. And somewhere deep inside of you, you are the same. Bishop will see that in you, and he will destroy you, Kiera."

She rose up on her haunches before me, her eyes locked with mine.

"Please, Kiera, you don't have to do this… you're breaking my heart," I whispered.

I looked into her eyes, and the brightness seemed to fade. It was like something I had said had made a connection with her.

"You don't have to be like the other wolves, Kiera," I breathed, sensing that the fight had gone out of her. "You might not be the Kiera Hudson I fell in love with, but you are the same. I know it."

Kiera lowered her claws and looked at me.

She opened her jaws to say something…

Clack! Clack! Clack!

Kiera jerked forward and I caught her in my arms. She howled in pain as she started to change. The soft black hair that had covered her body fell away, revealing the real Kiera hidden beneath. Her hazel eyes were open as she looked blankly up into my face. I cradled her in my arms and held her tight, and it was then I saw the circular red bullet hole in her forehead. A line of thick, black blood trickled from it and down onto her cheek. It looked like she was crying tears of blood.

"Kiera," I cried, holding her lifeless body to my chest.

A shadow fell over us. I looked up to see a hooded figure standing before me. In one hand was a gun, and in the other there was a camera.

"You shot her!" I cried. *"You killed her!"*

Slowly, the photographer pulled back the hood.

"No!" I gasped, seeing the photographer's face. "Why did you have to kill Kiera?"

"To save your life, Potter," the photographer said.

Dead Lost

(Kiera Hudson Series Two)
Book 8
Coming Soon!

Also available by Tim O'Rourke

'Vampire Shift' (Kiera Hudson Series One Book 1)
'Vampire Wake' (Kiera Hudson Series One Book 2)
'Vampire Hunt' (Kiera Hudson Series One Book 3)
'Vampire Breed' Kiera Hudson Series One Book 4)
'Wolf House' (Kiera Hudson Series One Book 4.5)
'Vampire Hollows' (Kiera Hudson Series One Book 5)
'Dead Flesh' (Kiera Hudson Series Two Book 1)
'Dead Night' (Kiera Hudson Series Two Book 1.5)
'Dead Angels' (Kiera Hudson Series Two Book 2)
'Dead Statues' (Kiera Hudson Series Two Book 3)
'Dead Seth' (Kiera Hudson Series Two Book 4)
'Dead Wolf' (Kiera Hudson Series Two Book 5)
'Black Hill Farm' (Book 1)
'Black Hill Farm: Andy's Diary' (Book 1)
'Doorways' (The Doorways Trilogy Book 1)
'The League of Doorways' (The Doorways Trilogy Book 2)
'Vampire Seeker' (Samantha Carter Series Book 1)
'Moonlight' (The Moon Trilogy Book 1)
'Moonbeam' (The Moon Trilogy Book 2)
'Witch' (A Sydney Hart novel) Book 1
'Yellow' (A Sydney Hart Novel) Book 2
You can contact Tim O'Rourke at
www.kierahudson.com Or by email at kierahudson91@aol.com

Printed in Great Britain
by Amazon.co.uk, Ltd.,
Marston Gate.